The Day My Grandfather
Was a Hero

Also by Paulus Hochgatterer in English translation

The Sweetness of Life (2008)
The Mattress House (2012)

Paulus Hochgatterer

The Day My Grandfather
Was a Hero

Translated from the German by
Jamie Bulloch

MACLEHOSE PRESS
QUERCUS · LONDON

First published as *Der Tag, an dem mein Grossvater ein Held war*
by Deuticke im Paul Zsolnay Verlag, Vienna, in 2017

First published in Great Britain in 2020 by

MacLehose Press
An imprint of Quercus Publishing Ltd
Carmelite House
50 Victoria Embankment
London EC4Y 0DZ

An Hachette UK company

The translation of this work was supported by a grant from the
Austrian Federal Ministry of Education Arts and Culture

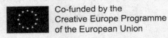

Co-funded by the
Creative Europe Programme
of the European Union

This publication has been funded with support from the European Commission. This
publication reflects the views only of the author, and the Commission cannot be held
responsible for any use which may be made of the information contained within.

10 9 8 7 6 5

Designed and typeset in Haarlemmer by Libanus Press Ltd
Printed and bound in Great Britain by Clays Ltd, Elcograf S.p.A.

MIX
Paper from
responsible sources
FSC® C104740

The state of exception is not equivalent to a dictatorship, but is a legal-free space, a zone of anomie in which all legal provisions – especially the distinction between what is public and private – are suspended.

Giorgio Agamben

The swallows are here. That happening can change every-thing. You're standing somewhere, outside the house for example, deep in thought or gazing at the clouds as you might on any other day, and after a while you notice that something's different. First you let your eyes wander along the horizon, over the hills, the roofs, the tops of the trees. Then you check for a whistling in the air, a hum or perhaps a smell. Finally you look to see whether you've torn a hole in your clothes without noticing, on a sleeve perhaps, on the knee or beneath an armpit. You can't see anything. Then you realise: the swallows have returned.

Otherwise everything is the same as it was yesterday. The clouds coursing across the sky, the molehills, the broken branches lying beneath the fruit trees, the nuthatch hopping up and down the wall of the barn. Nuthatches are lucky, Laurenz says, just like tortoises or hedgehogs or stag beetles. Magpies and foxes bring bad luck, he says. The swallows dart down, making loops between the barn and the stable. These are the ones with white bellies and V-shaped tails, not those with forked tails and red throats. Barn swallows, house martins. It's silly how I always get them mixed up. Occasionally they perch on the ridge of the barn roof for a few seconds. I can't remember now whether swallows are supposed to bring good or bad luck.

I return to the house, climb the stairs, turn right into the girls' room and take from the cupboard one of the brown notebooks, a pencil and the little pocketknife with the horn handle. Nobody sees me. Back downstairs and outside. From the barn door I run diagonally across the meadow to the garden, along the picket fence and then up the hill between the fields. Right at the top, next to a stunted blackthorn, I spin around, and again, and again. Then I sit on the grass. Here, right beside the bush, the ground is almost always dry. I look around. From here I can see everything. This is my place.

They say my name is Nelli. Sometimes I believe them, sometimes I don't. Sometimes I think my name is Elisabeth or Katharina. Or Isolde, like the young sales assistant in the hat shop. She's the reason I go into town from time to time. When I stand outside the shop and peer through the window, I see Isolde's torso floating around inside, back and forth along the shelves. The head with its auburn plait floats on top. I can't see anything from the waist down. I imagine her lower half having sat itself down somewhere. Perhaps all the toing and froing has become too exhausting. Perhaps it doesn't like the plait or the way in which the upper half says, How may I help you? But I don't tell anyone these sorts of things.

They say I'm thirteen years old and that there's a document, or more precisely a piece of paper with a stamp, showing my name and date of birth. I don't care about my birthday. Nobody celebrates birthdays here. Name days, yes; birthdays, no. Nobody knows when my name day is. Whenever I ask they just shrug. Whenever I ask about school they get nervous. Laurenz says that people do have to learn, but everything in good time. At the moment, he says, it's best for everyone if I wait a while before going to school. I don't know what's really best for me.

There are some things I'm certain of. I've been here for one hundred and forty-six days. I have a plan. Sometimes I lie.

On the third or fourth day I started making tally marks in my first brown notebook, on the last page, one for every day. Four vertical lines and one across, bunches of five. "How do you know how to do that?" Laurenz asked. "No idea," I said. "Like a fighter pilot," he said. He was the one who gave me the notebook, because I looked like the kind of person who enjoyed writing, he said. He used to look like that when he was younger too, he told me, which was why they sent him to the seminary and then he became a writer at the front. In the middle of winter he would sit in the bunker writing daily reports. He cut off the tips of the right thumb and index finger of his woollen glove to give him a better grip on the pencil. That's the only thing that really interests me about his story. I find everything else – snow and bayonets and man against man – really dull. I talked to Antonia, who promised to knit me gloves with fingertips you can fold back. She's in the fourth year of secondary school and knits so beautifully you would think her things were made in a factory.

I'm squatting on my heels, just looking. The roofs of the town, three church towers, the town hall, the hill where the rows of fruit trees meet, the beech wood, the neighbouring houses, the ditch with the fire pond and the beehives. Far to the south, the mountains. The Sonntagberg, the Hochkogel, the Ötscher. That's what they say. Every mountain has its own place and every mountain has its own name. There's a church up on the Sonntagberg, you can see it very clearly.

Just now the sky is empty. The sun and the clouds don't count. The moon and the stars wouldn't count either. Aeroplanes count, as do geese that fly in a wedge formation, and buzzards when they circle up above. Swallows would count too, but I can't see any at the moment.

Annemarie is coming. I can hear her rapid, slightly uneven footsteps on the gravel path. Then she stops. I focus on the spot where the path meets the brow of the hill. The first thing that comes into view is Annemarie's parting, her dark-blonde hair combed tightly to the side. It's plaited behind the ears. The ears themselves stick out like little wings. The sleeveless tunic with its flowery pattern and buttons that are mere decoration. Six tiny, light-blue buttons that are sewn on and don't actually button anything up. The satchel straps over her shoulders. Noticing me sitting there, she lifts her head. Her face is triangular, blotchy and wet. I get up. "What's wrong?" I ask. She doesn't respond. "Why are you crying?"

Everyone calls her "Little One", even though she's actually quite tall for her eight years, the second tallest in her class, she says. She's the youngest of the five sisters, which must be where Little One comes from. Grete, Katharina, Antonia, Roswitha and Annemarie – the five sisters. I worked out who was who after a few days. All five girls look like their mother. "Nature decided against the father," Laurenz says. Why does a girl need to look like her father, I wonder, but I don't say anything. "Leo looks a bit like his father," Laurenz says. That's not much use to the father, however, for Leo isn't here at the moment. Leo, the only son.

Annemarie stands there, staring past me, tears running down her cheeks. "What's wrong?" I say again. She's shaking from head to toe. "Nothing," she says. I imagine Frau Gretz, her teacher, calling her up to the blackboard and making her write sentences like *The narcissi are flowering magnificently* or *Even the apple tree is now blossoming*. I imagine Annemarie spelling narcissi with three "s"s and blossoming with only one. I picture Gretz in her grey suit with the badge on the lapel, looking fat and red in the face. Bamboo pointer in hand, she plants herself in front of Annemarie, and right now it doesn't matter one bit that at home she has a husband whose legs have been shot off and a mother who can't remember her daughter's name and who sometimes eats bird food. She raises the bamboo stick and whacks it fiercely on the teacher's desk. I imagine the echo lingering in the classroom for a second and at that moment it's all up with Annemarie.

I take her in my arms. "Was it Gretz?" I ask. She shakes her head. "Did she shout at you?" I ask. I imagine Gretz summoning to the blackboard all those she knows are slightly unsure of themselves, making them write *blossoming*, *narcissi* and *magnificently*, then shouting and making fun of them. I lay my face on Annemarie's head and sniff her hair. "You can sleep in my bed tonight," I say, and I imagine us lying on our sides, her in front, and feeling her back, which is as narrow as a young goat's, with her head smelling of forest and her neck of milk.

"Did she make you write 'narcissi'?" I ask, and when she shakes her head again I say, "Was it something else? Did you see something? Did you go to the railway? Did you peer into the bomb crater?" Sometimes they throw things into the bomb crater like junk or dead animals. "Was there an air-raid warning?" I ask, "or did you bump into someone, a stranger?" She looks right through me and says nothing.

"Come on, let's go," I say. We take the path through the ditch, which means you approach the farmhouse from below. For a while it disappears from view, then, after the fire pond, it suddenly emerges again, first the red roof, then the upstairs windows, then the entire house. I like it when things appear like that. I tell Annemarie how she pointed out Gretz to me one Sunday in church, how my immediate impression was that this woman sitting on the far left in her tight, grey suit only wished the worst on everyone else, and how after Mass Laurenz said, "Gretz looks like an anti-aircraft gun."

We walk past the elderflower bushes by the pond. A few tits are hopping on the branches. On the path is the skin of a grass snake. As I take a big step over it, Annemarie suddenly says, "Agnes came to get me again." "Which Agnes?" I say, even though I know the answer. Annemarie stops.

Annemarie tells me that Agnes was waiting outside the house, a smock over her black dress, her hair beneath the dark-blue scarf with silver stripes, as always. First she asked whether Annemarie wanted to see the two calves that had been born the day before, twin calves, that doesn't happen very often. When Annemarie said no, they had a new-born calf of their own on the farm, Agnes grabbed her by the arms. Annemarie stops and looks at me. "And then she said I had to go inside with her," she tells me. "She said I was a good girl and she didn't dare go in on her own anymore, and then she told me that one day he would kill her or himself." "Who is *he*?" I ask. I know the answer to this too.

She didn't dare protest. When she entered the house with Agnes, nobody else was there. Agnes looked around anxiously, she tells me, then hurried her into the parlour, right beneath the picture that hangs above the dining table in there. She shoved Annemarie onto the bench and sat beside her. "She said she wanted another child," Annemarie tells me, "she said she's entitled to it and this time it doesn't have to be a boy like Rudi." Then she said that Annemarie was the sort of girl a mother would cherish: clean, helpful and a quick learner. Rudi was like this too, a particularly quick learner, you could see it in his eyes. He was able to write his name, even though he hadn't started school yet. She knew that Annemarie could already write lots of things, and she could read and was good at geography and knew her times tables.

The wind wafts through the ditch. The young leaves of the birches shine yellow. If you don't look too closely you might think they're blossoms. This is one of those moments when you expect to meet someone on the path, a man, or at least a rabbit. But nobody comes our way.

Annemarie wipes her cheeks on her sleeve. "I don't like the photograph," she says. "Which photograph?" I ask. "The one of Rudi," she says. "His jumper is ugly and his trousers are really baggy and he looks at you as if he's not really there." There's truth in that, I think, but I don't say it out loud. Annemarie is as white as a sheet. In the end, she tells me, Agnes asked her if she knew what adoption was. She said, yes, adoption was for children who didn't have parents, and Agnes said basically that was true, but it could also work the other way around.

The kitchen has three windows, one facing east and two facing south. Through these windows broad shafts of light angle into the room. The flour in the air makes everything shimmer as in a fairy story. I'm sitting beside the door to the parlour on an old, dark-brown chair with an openwork back rest in the shape of a heart. "Does flour have a smell?" I ask.

The farmer's wife is kneading dough and sweating. Antonia is taking large strides up and down the kitchen, reciting a poem out loud. It begins with a castle in Alsace, which is well known to legend. I've no idea why she's doing this. Two days ago it was announced that school was cancelled until further notice, even after the Easter holidays. Antonia said she couldn't understand why as the secondary school building was completely intact. It hadn't been hit by a bomb and there weren't any cracks in the walls. Only the building beyond it, with the butcher's on the ground floor, had been hit. As well as a butcher's assistant. They say all you could see was his head, peering above the rubble. He'd been covered in a layer of red-brick dust.

"What does flour smell of?" I ask. Antonia stops her

marching, turns and stares at me. "That's the stupidest question I've ever heard!" she hisses. The farmer's wife looks up. "Don't fight," she says. With a knife she divides the dough into eight lumps, then kneads them one by one, dusting them occasionally with flour and slapping each one of them hard against the kneading board.

"Why are you bothering to learn a poem by heart when there's no more school?" I say to Antonia. "Shut your trap!" she says, then starts striding back and forth again, her plaits flying about. Without wanting to I take note of every line she says. *She crossed the woods with a few quick steps.* It irritates me, but there's nothing I can do about it.

"Grandmother...?" I try to ask the farmer's wife something. "I said, keep your trap shut!" Antonia interrupts me. Rather than mention the poem again, I ask her when she's going to get around to knitting me the gloves with the fingertips you can fold back. "Only the right hand," I say. "You can forget it!" she says. And besides, for the hundredth time now, her mother is not my grandmother. "Leave the poor girl alone," the farmer's wife tells Antonia. "She's not trying to say 'mother'." A mother is a gift, she adds, and anybody lucky enough to still have one ought to be happy. But 'grandmother' is wrong, Antonia insists. None of her sisters has a child, nor to her knowledge does Leo. So grandmother is categorically wrong.

One after the other, the farmer's wife flours the eight

flat straw baskets which are leaning up against the wall behind the kneading board. She forms the lumps of dough into balls, places them in the baskets, huddles the baskets together and covers them all with a large blue cloth.

The longer the poem goes on, the more often Antonia has to consult her book. By the end she's just reading it. "You will not find them" – that's the last line. I imagine a wicked person turning up, a Russian or a man with a rifle, and putting Antonia into the oven instead of the bread dough. Maybe he wraps her in the blue cloth beforehand so you can't see the terror in her face. But I want my gloves before that happens.

"You know what happened to her mother," the farmer's wife says. Wiping her hands on her apron, she sits at the table with the proving baskets. Antonia stares at the wall. "Nobody knows that," she says, "not even she does." "She can't know," the farmer's wife says. "She suffered some sort of blast injury to her head." "She's soft in the head," Antonia says. "She knows nothing, and if she says she does she's lying." The farmer's wife tells Antonia she ought to watch it – jealous people sin easily. Then, before you know it, you're in Purgatory, right at the back. "Either she knows nothing or she lies," Antonia repeats. Now she looks me in the eye. Her eyebrows are darker than her hair and there's a slight curve to her parting. It's strange, sometimes you like people even though they say bad things about you.

The farmer's wife says she remembers October 17th very well. It was a cold, rainy Tuesday. As usual that morning she was loading the milk churns onto the cart with her husband and Laurenz, to take them to the collection point, when all of a sudden there was this noise in the sky. The three of them stood by the gate and listened. "Like bees swarming," the farmer said. Then, a few minutes later, when they heard the first strikes: "Like beaters flushing out game." After a while, she says, Laurenz shook his head and said, "That's not bees, that's the British over the Niebelungen factory. Lancasters, twenty of them at least, perhaps thirty." Lancasters, she remembered, were like Messerschmitts.

By now, Antonia says, she knows every word of the story. Two days later I appeared, like a ghost. Katharina was out in the field, harvesting fodder beet with the horse. On her way home she found me sitting there on the cart, silent and caked in mud. "That's right, silent and caked in mud," the farmer's wife says. "In a dark-blue factory coat, far too thin for that cold day, trembling hands and blue lips and blah blah blah," Antonia says, slapping the windowsill when she finishes her sentence. Why, for heaven's sake, does she need to hear this dismal story yet again? "Maybe one day she'll be able to remember," the farmer's wife says. "Even you don't believe that," Antonia says.

Now I could tell the story to its conclusion. How for

days they asked me my name and about my family, but I didn't utter a single word. How I stared wide-eyed, as if I'd met the Devil himself, and how, after they'd given up trying, I said in response to Roswitha's question as to whether I could remember anyone else, perhaps a neighbour, "Yes, Frau Schwertner."

On that October 17th, two large blocks housing factory workers, right beside the Niebelungen factory in Herzograd, Sankt Valentin, were bombed to rubble. One of the tenants, whose dead body they recovered a few days later, was Marie Schwertner, an unmarried typist from the factory's payroll accounts department. In the apartment next to hers a Danube Swabian family by the name of Deinhardt, who had only recently moved in, had perished beneath the rubble: mother, father and two sons. They hadn't found the daughter, Cornelia, thirteen years old, nor had she turned up anywhere else.

Because the coat I was wearing when Katharina put me on the cart had a sewn-on Niebelungen factory badge, Grandfather – the farmer – went to the local authority to find out whether I might have been reported missing. Two days later a reply to his enquiry arrived by cable from Sankt Valentin. My description matched that of the missing Cornelia Deinhardt, who in view of the sad circumstances was henceforth to be treated as an orphan and placed in state care. Because of the threat level they requested the local welfare office here to refrain from sending the girl back to Sankt Valentin, instead to entrust her until further notice to the care of the family of Jakob and Barbara Leithner. Compensation for expenditure incurred would naturally be forthcoming. As the girl currently lacked proof of identity, the registry office here was kindly requested to provide a provisional identity document, thank you, Heil Hitler.

Grandfather put the piece of paper with my name, date of birth and the official stamp on the table in the parlour and nodded silently when Grandmother asked if I now belonged to them. Grandmother folded up the document and uttered just one sentence: "Here, we're going to call her Nelli."

I could say all of this, but I don't. Instead I say, "I don't think I'll ever remember, everything in my head was bombed away." Antonia snaps at me. "Liar!" she shouts, before running outside.

I sit there quietly, wondering whether flour makes a sound as it dances in the air. The farmer's wife has her hands clasped and she's looking at the blue cloth. "She's in a muddle," she says after a while. "You have to understand that." Everything's going to pieces, she says, now there's not even school anymore. Not to mention Leo. Out of all of them Antonia feels closest to him. "Agnes Hürner wants to adopt Annemarie," I tell her, because I can't think of anything better to say right now. "I know," the farmer's wife says. "She told me."

"And?"

"No 'and'. She hasn't got an easy life either." Ever since the thing with their boy, Agnes' husband Stefan has been going to pieces regularly, she says. And that's why he hasn't had to join up yet. A neurologist wrote an assessment saying he might represent a danger to his comrades. Stefan didn't have to join up, but Leo did, she says. And yet it would be far more logical to send a madman into this mad war. At least that's what Laurenz says when there are no strangers listening, she tells me.

"Will you tell me a martyr story afterwards?" I ask. At first the farmer's wife looks surprised, then she laughs. "You and your martyr stories," she says. "I'll need my notebook for that," I say and run off.

When I return everything is different. The farmer's wife is sitting there, both hands clutching the edge of the table, Antonia rigid beside her. Standing in the middle of the kitchen is a man I don't know. He's wearing grey loden knee breeches and a swastika armband. He's short, fat and bald. "Well, well, who do we have here?" he says when he sees me. I stand by the wall and look at the farmer's wife. She's deathly pale. "Cornelia Deinhardt," Antonia says.

"Aha, Deinhardt," the man says, scrutinising me.

"A victim of the Sankt Valentin bombing. She's with

us now." Antonia looks innocently at the man, but I sense that what she'd most like to do is stick a knife into his throat. The man grins. "I thought that..." he says. "From a Danube Swabian family whose apartment was bombed," the farmer's wife says. "The only one who survived." "Alright," the man says, no longer grinning. He says he's come to talk about something completely different. "Where's the farmer?" he asks. "In the field," the wife says. "Why do you ask?" "Because of the blackout," the man says.

"What about the blackout?" the farmer's wife says. The man takes a piece of paper from his trouser pocket and unfolds it. "We've received a statement," he says.

"What sort of statement?"

"'The house shines in the dark like a chandelier'," he reads. "That's the message."

Antonia leaps up. "Such nonsense," she exclaims. "Shines like a chandelier – you'd have to set light to it to make it do that!" The farmer's wife grabs her by the arm. "Who reported us?" she asks. That's irrelevant, the man says, a statement is a statement. He puts the piece of paper back in his trouser pocket and rocks forwards and backwards on the soles of his feet. Surely they must understand, he says, what his obligations were in relation to such incidents. Hopefully they also understood what this could mean for a farm that in times like these enjoyed the privilege of two male workers. "That's a lie," Antonia hisses.

"Which bastard reported us?" "Be quiet!" the farmer's wife says. She motions to the man to stay where he is and hurries out of the kitchen.

First the man lifts the blue cloth to look at the baskets with the bread dough, then he points his finger at me. "Where are you from?" he says. "From Sankt Valentin," I say.

"I know that. I mean, originally. Where does your family come from?"

"Reşiţa," I say.

"Reşiţa?" He doesn't have a clue.

"Reşiţa, not far from Timişoara," I say. "In the Banat."

"In the Banat? What do they speak there?"

"German," I say. "The Danube Swabians speak German."

"Is Reşiţa on the Danube?"

"No," I say. "But almost."

"What do you mean by *almost*?"

"Severin is on the Danube. That's a different town. An hour away by train."

I notice Antonia gawping at me as if I were a ghost.

"So Reşiţa has a railway, does it?" the man asks. At that moment the farmer's wife comes back. She's carrying a bundle covered in a checked dishcloth, which she places in the man's hands. "There," she says. "Now go." The man feels the bundle. "I'll make one final exception," he says. "An absolutely final exception."

"Of course Reşiţa has a railway," I say, "and there are

even fast trains." The man gives me another stare. "And a synagogue?" he says. "Does Reşiţa have a synagogue too?"

"What's a synagogue?" I ask.

The farmer's wife approaches the man and lays a hand on his shoulder. "Please go now," she says. "I have to take the embers out of the oven. Otherwise the bread won't work."

When the man has gone, Antonia is still gawping at me. "What was all that about?" she asks. "What was what about?" I ask back. "Reşiţa, Banat, Danube Swabians," she says. "Can you remember all of a sudden?"

"No," I say. "First, I'm a liar, as you keep saying, and second I paid attention in geography. Banat, Vojvodina, Lesser Wallachia, Greater Wallachia – I learned all that."

Antonia looks away, then mutters something about the bastards who report people to get them sent to the front or to Dachau. Looking seriously worried, the farmer's wife tells Antonia to be very careful what she says to certain people – because of Dachau.

I sit at the table and open my notebook. The farmer's wife sits opposite me. "Catherine, Lucy or Bartholomew?" she asks.

"Bartholomew," Laurenz says. Suddenly he's standing in the doorway in rubber galoshes and the black apron he always wears when he's working, his hair dishevelled.

When we all look at him, he says, "Some people deserve to be skinned."

"Lucy rather than Bartholomew," I say. He laughs. "Yes, some people deserve to have their eyes poked out too," he says. He's pale and his breathing is shallow, like a dog's.

The Story of the Boy
Who Didn't Drown

It was the Sunday after Corpus Christi when Rudi Hürner fell into the millstream, but in the end didn't drown. The previous Thursday, Corpus Christi itself, had been under water too, which first nobody could have anticipated in the middle of June, and second was a tragedy for the little boy, just four years old. His parents had told him daily about the coming procession, about the young birch trees which would decorate the whole town, the sumptuous altars on the main street, the brass music and the baskets from which children would strew flowers: peonies, snapdragons and marguerites. In the end Rudi became fixated by the idea of the canopy which his parents had told him was carried expressly for the priest and the Blessed Sacrament. He'd assumed that he would be allowed to strew flowers like the other children, and that they would put him in one of those white dresses that his mother had kept talking about with such excitement. The girls who'd taken their First Communion a few weeks earlier would wear their white dresses and marguerites in their hair, she'd said.

On the morning of Corpus Christi, Rudi had stood in

the parlour in the white frock Agnes had made for him from a few metres of cotton batiste and tulle, holding a wicker basket filled with dark-red peonies, howling that he didn't want rain, he wanted to strew flowers and watch the canopy being carried around the town. His father tried to appease him by saying that nobody had wanted it to pour down; he could scatter flowers here in the parlour and next year the weather would surely be fine. None of this softened the child's rage, quite the opposite in fact, and in despair Stefan Hürner then said something which later would almost turn out to be disastrous: "If it's not raining next Sunday, we'll drive to church on the tractor." Agnes looked at him in sheer horror – not because she herself would walk there, but because from the very day her husband had acquired the green Deutz half a year earlier she'd regarded it as the Devil's work: loud, smelly and dangerous.

"No rain," Rudi said when he looked out of the window on the Sunday morning. When, in response to his mother's remark that it wasn't something you could tell with much accuracy from inside, he stepped outside to make sure. "No rain," he said again. "Well, then," said Stefan Hürner, who hadn't for one second entertained the idea that his son might have forgotten the promise, "get dressed." "Where's the frock?" Rudi said. He certainly wasn't going to ride on a tractor in a white frock, his father said, and in any case, white frocks and baskets of flowers were only allowed on Corpus Christi. "Besides, you'd freeze to death on the way there in that flimsy thing," Agnes said. Despite his protests, they put the boy in his dark-brown corduroys and the woolly jumper she'd knitted for him for Christmas.

"Don't drive too quickly," she instructed her husband as she lifted Rudi up. Laughing, Stefan took hold of the boy and sat him between his legs. Rudi beamed. "Tractor," he said. "That's it, our green tractor," Stefan said.

They drove into town on the main road, swerving around a goat that was blocking the way, greeting all the church-goers on foot and overtaking several horse-drawn carts. Each time he shifted up into fourth gear, Stefan called out, "Top speed!" and Rudi laughed out loud. When they passed a howitzer from which the artillery piece had been removed, Rudi first asked whether he could have a cannon too, and then who was going to win the war. "We are, of course," Stefan said.

He parked the Deutz by the graveyard wall. Two women walking past whispered, then one of them asked the boy if he could drive a tractor himself yet. Rudi took his father's hand and turned away without saying anything.

Beneath the chestnut trees that lined a short avenue leading to the church, his father explained that this was the last section of the Corpus Christi route. "Can I drive a tractor in the Corpus Christi procession?" Rudi asked. "Tractors are too loud for that," Stefan said.

It's hard to say what induced Stefan Hürner to drive to the wetlands after Sunday Mass. Perhaps it was the sight of his wife who'd appeared in church at the last moment and squeezed herself into the second row on the women's side diagonally opposite him, visibly worked up and distraught, a trait he sometimes liked in young women. Perhaps it was his son's excitement, his way of asking questions, holding his head in the wind or imitating the priest's gestures during Mass. Maybe it had something to do with the weather, too, and the pleasure to be had in the boisterous sounds of the new tractor. At any rate, when they stepped out onto the church forecourt with the other young people after the blessing, he announced that on the way back he wanted to pass by the wetlands to look at a couple of pastures he owned there. Agnes looked at him in surprise. "They'll be ready to mow in a week's time, and the feed is worth as little this year as ever," she told him. He intended to go there all the same, Stefan said. Rudi said he would come too. Agnes rolled her eyes, muttered something about men and gave in.

Steering well clear of the camp at Allersdorf, they made their way to the Ybbs wetlands on farm tracks. They came across a buzzard on a post, a pair of storks and a herd of seven or eight deer. The boy didn't pay attention to any of these even though his father pointed them all out. Rudi was absorbed instead by holding the steering wheel. At regular intervals he would say, "Tractor," with satisfaction in his voice.

Beyond a copse of ash and hornbeam they arrived at the pastures which were the reason for the excursion. Along a length of perhaps one hundred and fifty metres the two parcels were separated by a dark, rapidly flowing and dead-straight stream. "The millstream," Stefan said as they crossed it over a plank bridge. "Will the tractor go under if it falls into the stream?" Rudi asked. "The tractor won't fall into the millstream," was Stefan's answer.

They drove along the edge of the larger pasture until they came to a cluster of field maples. In one of the trees a hide had been knocked up out of rough fir wood. Stefan stopped on the right of the pasture and switched off the engine. "I need to check the ladder," he said. "Will you come with me?" Rudi still had his hands on the wheel. "I'm staying here," he said. "Don't drive off, whatever you do," Stefan said, raising his index finger and laughing.

From that moment, in truth, the only recollection was of the trail that led through the tall grass like a narrow ditch, the bent bellflowers, the slight curve to the left at the beginning and finally, about two-thirds of the way there, a flat molehill with the tiny footprint in the middle of it. At the end of the trail, as if this had been the destination from the outset, stood a coppice willow. Its trunk, barely the height of a man, slanted obliquely from the embankment, extending to the middle of the stream.

Afterwards Stefan Hürner could not remember whether any part of the hide was damaged, the ladder or the planks, nor could he recall what he saw from the top, for example whether he had looked towards the tractor or not. He couldn't even say how long he'd spent up there, a minute or perhaps an hour, because sleep had got the better of him.

So there was just this trail, and of course the most likely course of events was that the boy had walked purposefully across the pasture, then kneeled down beside the willow, wrapping his left arm around the trunk so he could feel for the bed of the stream with his right hand. Unaware that the millstream on this pasture was a good metre and a half deep, he would have lost his balance and tipped forwards into the water. Not anticipating any danger, he wouldn't even have screamed. The surprise and the cold of the water would have momentarily taken his breath away. He would have thrashed around a few times, and soon his head would have been completely under water. The current would have whisked him away at once.

The boy's body would have rolled along the bed of the stream, rotating evenly, then it would have been washed back up to the surface, but the lack of meanders or inlets would have given it no opportunity to come ashore. After about a kilometre and a half, he would have been stopped by the grating at the arm of the canal leading to the madder mill. He would have been pushed upwards, the woollen jumper would have shone dark red and the two women cycling to the mill to buy powdered dye would have said that the boy in the water, his head facing the sky and his eyes closed, already looked as if he were lying on a bier.

The gendarmes would have arrived soon after Stefan Hürner, bringing the community doctor with them. All would have been utterly helpless in the face of the man's despair.

That was the most likely course of events.

Afterwards, Stefan Hürner would often tell how he got back to the tractor, called out for Rudi, and the moment he began walking along the trail in the pasture he pictured the drowned boy in his arms. He howled with fear and pain, he said, and raced towards the coppice willow. He fell to his knees, staring like a fool into the water, for a while completely failing to notice the soaking-wet boy sitting on the pasture on the bank opposite. "I'm wet," Rudi called out. Stefan said that he waded straight into the stream, not minding that the water came right up to his chest. "I'm wet," Rudi said again. Then the boy told his father how he'd lost his balance and toppled into the stream. All of a sudden, he said, a young woman with dark hair and a blue coat appeared and pulled him out. "And so I didn't drown," the boy said finally. "Mama's going to be really pleased," Stefan said, unable to think of anything better.

March 20th, 1945

They've been flying since early morning. The weather is fine, which means that you can see them too: tiny crosses, flashing silver between the clouds. The squadrons vary in size: the first two were smaller, but the one passing now is enormous.

I lean against the wall, at arm's length from the farmer. He's peering through his binoculars at the sky and counting under his breath. He stops when he gets to forty. "Americans," he says. "I think they're Americans." If Laurenz were here he'd say, "Eighteen Flying Fortresses, twelve Lancasters, ten Mosquitos and a few Lightnings." To which I'd reply, "There are four Manchesters among them too, and at least two Heinkels." He'd say, "Someone's acting like she knows what she's talking about – Heinkels, what side are they on?" and I'd say, "They're ours, that was just a test."

"Americans – is that a good thing or a bad thing?" Katharina asks. She flits around as if she's scared, moving things from here to there, a wooden rake, a milk pail and a white tablecloth that she folds as she walks. "Depends," the farmer says. Then he says it must be Linz's turn, most likely the steelworks and Danube bridge. "They're not stupid," he says. "They know where to drop their loads."

Linz is a strange name for a city, just like Oslo or Brussels or Vladivostok. I imagine Linz to be full of very determined people who stride along the streets in suits or clothes made of quality material, and who know what needs to be done. Vladivostok I picture as an expansive harbour with thousands of seals swimming in it. I don't know why. I've never been to Linz or Vladivostok.

I don't get around to wondering what I imagine Brussels and Oslo to be like because the farmer suddenly lets out a groan, pushes off from the wall with his back and takes a few steps forwards, still looking through the binoculars, as if intent on walking all the way to what he can see. "What is it?" I ask, and at that moment I hear both the droning and the sirens. The farmer points wordlessly at the sky. At right angles to the squadrons high in the sky comes a group of dark, four-engine aircraft from the north. They're flying much lower, comfortably beneath the clouds. "What are they doing?" I say. "Get inside," the farmer says. I shake my head. "I want to watch," I protest.

"Everyone inside – now!"

"But I want to watch."

All of a sudden Katharina is beside me, she takes hold of my right wrist, gives me a slap and drags me into the house. Katharina has never hit me before, not even in jest.

I think she likes me. She's the second eldest and almost as tall as her father. In the distance artillery fire starts up, followed soon afterwards by the first muffled explosions. "They're heading for the city," the farmer says. "The camp, maybe, or the station." Then he tells me of the fighter planes that accompany the bomber squads, and that some pilots take pleasure in shooting at people on the ground. A tinsmith's assistant was killed like this. During an air-raid alert he was carrying a section of galvanised guttering across the yard, when suddenly a British Spitfire appeared directly overhead. The pilot gave the trigger of his onboard machine gun a brief squeeze and that was all it needed. One bullet in the thigh, one in the stomach and one right in the middle of the neck, the tinsmith said. He'd watched the whole thing from his workshop. The aircraft had swooped vertically down from the sky like a falcon, he said, silently and accurately. After firing its rounds at the assistant the Spitfire had disappeared northwards in an elegant arc over the Danube. Fortunately, the farmer said, the tinsmith's assistant was already sixty-two. He'd lived his life, but those bullets could just as easily have killed a really young man.

Annemarie is sitting at the table in the parlour, her eyes closed and hands over her ears. "It won't last for ever," Katharina says. Annemarie screws up her eyes even more tightly. I sit beside her. "Agnes Hürner isn't going to adopt you," I say after a while. Katharina looks at me sternly.

"What are you talking about?" she says. Annemarie opens her eyes. "How do you know that?" she says. "I just do," I say.

"How?"

"Just do."

"You're lying!"

"I wrote it down," I say. "I'll show you." When I get up to fetch my notebook, Annemarie takes her hands off her head. Her ears stick out like little wings. It's silly, but I can't help thinking the same thing each time I see her ears.

Laurenz is standing at the top of the stairs in his flannel nightgown, holding on tight to the banisters. "They're bombing the city," I say, because nothing else comes to mind. "I can hear," he says. "I need my notebook," I say. "That can wait," he says, beckoning me into his bedroom. "I need you." His room is neat and tidy. I've seen these things before: the wardrobe, the bureau with the porcelain horse on it, the slim glass cabinet with books, and the two framed photographs on the wall, one of his parents' wedding, the other a desert landscape with a group of people and two dromedaries.

"I've never been a farmer," Laurenz said when he invited me into this room for the first time a few months ago and I looked slightly surprised. "I may be the eldest but I've never been a farmer. I was always more interested in crazy ideas than in the soil or the weather. But I was too godless to be a priest and too impatient to be a teacher. So I became a crazy farmhand who reads books. Another alternative." He gave a bitter laugh and I remember feeling fairly sad at the time. But I'll never tell him that.

Laurenz pulls over the chair by the bureau for himself and gestures that I should sit on the bed. I do so, even though I feel uncomfortable. I don't like sitting on beds. Laurenz has pale-green eyes, hair which is more white than grey, and a long, thin scar on his left cheek. His fingertips are brown. He sticks out his right hand as if he were going to lay it on my forearm, but he doesn't. Whenever I don't know what to expect, I watch very carefully.

Laurenz begins to talk. From time to time he props his arms on his thighs, falls silent and just breathes.

"You're a smart girl, and I'm a stupid old man." This is the first thing he says. "I know the Grim Reaper will be coming for me soon," he continues with a grin. He talks about the rottenness eating him up from within, and how after the X-rays the doctor stood by the screen with the images of his chest, pointing with a bamboo cane at various white spots and just saying, "There, there, there, there and there." He says he doesn't know if the value of a life can be measured by how many people one has seen die, or how many one has made happy; and he says that pain is always relative. He would bet a fortune, he says, that dying from white spots is more comfortable than dying over hot coals.

As an expert on martyrdom I ought to know this. I'd like to tell him I'm not an expert on martyrdom, but then I think of the term he just used – "Grim Reaper" – and my throat constricts.

Right now, all I can recall of the farmer's wife's story about St Lawrence is that it was originally about handing out money, about rich and poor people, justice and greed.

Laurenz coughs furiously a few times, goes grey in the face and wheezes. "You're not part of the family," he says once he recovers sufficiently, "which is a shame, but it makes some things simpler." He doesn't know how long he's got left, he says, and as he's assuming that I'll remain in this house, irrespective of my true identity, he's decided to confide a few things in me. "I'm a coward and you're tough enough," he says, and I'm not sure I understand what he means by that.

There's one thing he needs to tell me, he says. He doesn't feel particularly good about this, because it's only about lightening his own burden, but he can't help it. It's about the farmer, his brother. Jakob is someone, Laurenz says, who at Epiphany can tell how many more days of frost the barley needs or, from a glance at a pregnant cow's belly, how the calf is lying. In other words, he has a natural talent for farming. That apart – and he's sorry to have to put it this way – Jakob is as narrow-minded as a man could possibly be. He also suffers from highly complex anxieties, like seizures, and in all honesty, it's completely thanks to his wife that the farm hasn't slid from one financial catastrophe to the next. Barbara is Jakob's great fortune, he insists. "Without her he'd have been in a madhouse ages ago," Laurenz says. "Or he would have hanged himself." "Where?" I ask. "In Mauer-Öhling, in the institution there," he says, and I don't tell him that I was asking about something different.

"She is his great fortune, as are the girls," Laurenz says. Now he's going to show me three things that are very important to him. I have to promise that I won't tell the others until he's no longer alive. He puts his hand on the middle drawer of the bureau and looks at me. I picture the farmer wandering through the cart shed and the barn with a rope, then going down into the press and finally up to the granary. I nod. "Promise?" Laurenz says. I nod again and say, "I promise."

He takes two envelopes from the drawer, one white and the other light brown. I lean forwards. The brown envelope bears a Wehrmacht stamp with eagle and swastika, and is addressed to the farmer. The white one is blank apart from a large "W" in the upper right-hand corner. "'W' for will," Laurenz says, placing his left hand on the envelope. "I could have written LAURENZ JOSEF LEITHNER, LAST WILL AND TESTAMENT, but I would have found that a bit much." I look at his hand. His fingers are coarse, with gnarled knuckles.

The top part of his ring finger is missing. A cartwheel that ran over it many years ago – I know the story. I can't help but think of the Grim Reaper, the farmer in the granary, Annemarie, the aeroplanes in the sky and Katharina slapping me. I have the sudden feeling that things are getting mixed up in my head. "May I guess?" I say. Laurenz looks at me in astonishment. "What?" he asks. "Nothing," I say. I don't even know what he has to bequeath. "The cleverest girl gets everything," he continues. When he notices me starting to ponder this, he grins. "*Everything* can mean different things," he says, "and I don't have that much." I give him a searching look. Who is the cleverest? Antonia? Or Grete? Grete is so silent that I imagine only very few people know whether she's clever or not. Katharina? Never. "What is important is that you know where the document is," he says, returning the envelope to the drawer. He coughs and looks out of the window. Then he points to the other envelope. "This is more difficult," he says. When I reach for the envelope he puts a hand on it. "This is much more difficult," he says.

The letter arrived a few days before Christmas, he says. He was bringing logs into the house with the wheelbarrow when he bumped into the postman on the driveway. Without saying a word the postman gave him the envelope and their eyes met, so to speak, on the Wehrmacht stamp. Just as silently, Laurenz slipped the letter into the pocket of his apron. The postman clearly understood, wished Laurenz a happy Christmas and got back on his bicycle. Besides the Wehrmacht letter, Laurenz recalls that two Christmas cards arrived in the post that day, as well as a package from Annemarie's godmother.

He stacked the wood and refilled the kitchen stove, just like on any other day, Laurenz says. Then he stood beside the window in his bedroom, but he can't remember for how long. Eventually he was able to open the letter. Laurenz runs his finger along the name and address, line by line, then around the two Hitler symbols. His left eyelid twitches.

"On November 2nd, 1944, All Souls' Day, in a heroic battle in Hürtgenwald," he says. He memorised that. At the bottom of the page, as well as the Wehrmacht stamp, he saw the stamp of the 116th tank division. "A greyhound," Laurenz says. "A greyhound on a meadow – as if that made it any better."

To begin with he thought he'd tell Jakob and Barbara after the holiday. Now he knows he was wrong. "You get to the point where you realise there are things you're simply incapable of," he says. I really want to ask him to show me the greyhound stamp, but I don't dare.

For a time we say nothing. "What was he like?" I ask eventually. "Leo?" he says. "Simple and full of fear, just like his father." He used to enjoy wandering in the forest, Laurenz tells me, and he loved animals, especially horses and the two oxen. "Who's going to be the farmer now, then?" I ask. Laurenz doesn't answer me. After a while he stands and goes over to his wardrobe. There's something else he has to show me.

He wears the grey-green felt coat hanging on the far left of the clothes rail only when it's cold and snowy and he goes into town on the horse-drawn sleigh. I think the coat dates back to the first war, but I'm not sure. He pats it on both sides. "Remember where it is," he says, removing a long object from the inside pocket and placing it on the bureau. I bend forwards. At first glance it looks like a dwarf's rifle. "What is it?" I say. "Somebody has to know where it is," he says. "Will you remember?" I nod, then say again, "What is it?" He reaches into the left outer pocket of the coat and pulls out a small blue cardboard box. "The cartridges," he says. "Will you remember where they are?" I nod once more. "It looks like a dwarf's rifle," I say. "If anyone does anything to the girls, the crazy farmhand will stop reading his books," Laurenz says, knocking the box of bullets on the top of the bureau.

He shows me everything: how to cock the sawn-off shotgun with its two barrels; how to load the bullets; how to remove the safety catch; how to think of something insignificant; how to pull both triggers. There are people who can teach you things.

March 21st, 1945

I like it best when she draws up her legs a little and the entire length of her back is against me. Then she snores occasionally or smacks her lips quietly. I push my left arm beneath her armpit and feel her ribs up to the neck of her nightgown and then hang my fingertips on her collarbone. She's thin and warm like a kitten. Sometimes when she's asleep she puts her feet on the bridge of mine and it feels as if she's standing on me, and I'd like to swallow her up there and then, skin and hair too.

There is noise coming from below. It's still dark outside. I can see the stars through the window. I hear the front door open, footsteps, the voice of the farmer's wife, other voices. Carefully untangling myself from Annemarie, I pull off the blanket and climb out of bed. Just before I get to the door she sits bolt upright. I stop where I am and turn around. "Is she there?" she asks. "Who?" I say.

"Is she coming to fetch me?"

"No," I say. "She's not coming to fetch you. She doesn't need to anymore."

"Why not?" she says, and I tell her because I know. She calls me a liar and I say I'm not, I know for certain, I wrote it down in my notebook. She calls me a liar again and climbs out of bed. When she's standing beside me in the darkness I sense her looking at me. I'd really like to pick her up right now, but I know she's too heavy.

We go to the top of the stairs and listen. Several people are speaking at once. One man is talking very loudly. Someone's crying. "Will you come downstairs with me?" I say. Annemarie nods. She looks at me, then down at herself. "In our nightgowns?" she says. "No," I say.

I know almost everyone sitting around the table in the parlour, which is reassuring. They are: Herr Lenzinger, the fat omnibus driver, with his wife; Frau Maier and Frau Woitsch, our two neighbours from the house at 10 Ardagger Strasse; Frau Maier's daughter, who's a qualified kindergarten teacher but still lives with her mother; an old man who, like Frau Maier and Frau Woitsch, comes for milk every few days, but whose name I've forgotten; and the vet with his daughter Jutta.

Sitting on the left of the corner bench is a young man I've never seen before. He has long blond hair and reddish-blond stubble, and is so thin that he looks on the verge of starvation. He's wearing trousers and a coat made of filthy canvas. He has one arm around something that could be a pipe or a piece of fencepost. It reaches up to his shoulders when he's sitting, and it's wrapped in green oilcloth tied with a carrying strap. The man is as still as a statue and his eyes are fixed on the floor. "Who is that?" Annemarie asks me softly. "No idea," I say. "Someone whose house has been bombed or a spy." She wants to know why I say a spy, and I tell her it's because that's what I imagine a spy to look like.

The person crying is Frau Woitsch and the person doing the most talking is the vet. He usually talks a lot, like when he puts drops in the horses' eyes or sticks a trocar into the stomach of a bloated cow. Now he's talking about how on their first flyover yesterday the enemy aircraft bombed the north of the city, nobody knows why because that's where the schools and the new cemetery are, but absolutely no military targets. Then he says that a second wave, an hour later, bombed the station and the factories to the south of it. He says that the oil train destined for Linz, which had been stopped because of the impending bombardment, had for safety been shunted eastwards out of the station. After the second attack was over they thought their strategy had worked, he explains, but only two hours later, in the middle of the afternoon, a tiny formation of Allied fighter aeroplanes appeared from the north-west, flying very low. They headed straight for the station area where they shelled the oil train, setting it alight, one wagon after another, more than one hundred of them. Some of the wagons exploded like bombs and the glow of the fire still hangs over the city, he says. Now Frau Woitsch is crying loudly, apart from which the room is silent for several moments. "Was he on duty?" the vet asks eventually. Frau Maier looks at Frau Woitsch, nods and says yes, he worked in the signal box on the very outskirts of the station. Annemarie pinches me and says, "Who?" "What do you mean, 'who'?" I say back.

"Who was in the signal box?"

"No idea," I say.

Laurenz brings perry and a few glasses. He's wearing his work clothes as if it were the middle of the day. When he puts the jug on the table he turns to the young man. "What's that?" he asks, pointing to the object by his side. The man pulls it closer to him. "Nothing," he says. "A rifle?" Laurenz asks. "It could be an anti-tank rocket launcher." The lad was carrying the thing on his shoulder the whole time, the omnibus driver says. "You carry rocket launchers on your shoulder," Laurenz says.

The farmer's wife and Grete come into the parlour from the hallway and put two piles of blankets and sheets in a window recess. "Leave him be," the farmer's wife says. She asks the young man his name and he says, Mikhail. Mikhail what? she asks, he shrugs and she asks again. "Just Mikhail," he says. "Where do you come from, then?" she keeps probing. "Templin," he says. "Where's Templin?" she asks. He shrugs once more. She looks around the room. Nobody knows where Templin is, not even the vet. "Near Reşiţa,"

I say. "Templin is near Reşiţa, a bit to the east, twenty kilometres perhaps." The young man looks at me in astonishment, as does the vet. I don't know why I said that.

During the day they'd stayed hidden in the little wood beside Edla palace, Frau Maier's daughter says, because they didn't know whether the aircraft would return. They thought about where they might find shelter, and split into groups. Few words had been needed. In fact, everyone had been fairly quiet the whole time, even the children. They didn't notice the young man at first, then suddenly he was sitting with them, leaning against the trunk of an ash tree with his strange rocket launcher package laid across his legs. They saw at once that he was very thin, as if he hadn't enjoyed a proper meal in ages, and overall he gave the impression of being harmless. That's why nobody objected to his joining them.

"Are you hungry?" the farmer's wife asks. For a while Mikhail doesn't respond, then he nods. She sends Grete to fetch some bread and dripping. "What a good idea," Herr Lenzinger says. His wife digs her elbow into his side. She'd be grateful, the farmer's wife says, if everyone stopped their stupid talk of rifles and rocket launchers. People who go around with weapons like that look quite different. If Mikhail has no objections, one of the children, Annemarie or Jutta perhaps, could pick the thing up. Mikhail looks up in horror. "Just pick it up," the farmer's wife says.

"I'm not doing it," Annemarie says. "Why not?" I ask. "Because he's a spy," she says. "He's not a spy," I say. "Yes, he is," she says, "you said so yourself." The farmer's wife asks where she got that idea from, and Annemarie says he looks just like a spy from Reşiţa: filthy and with a beard like that. "From Templin," I say. "Same difference," she says.

"You do it, then," the vet says to his daughter. Jutta knits her brow, then looks at her father questioningly. "He's not a spy," he says, pushing her off the bench. She's half a head shorter than Annemarie and she's wearing a dark-blue duster jacket. She makes her way tentatively around the table. In the end she stands there, eyes to the floor. "Go on!" the vet says. She doesn't move.

Mikhail abruptly bends forwards, grabs Jutta's forearms and pulls her hands to either side of the oilcloth. "Pick it up," he says. "Go on!" She's quite clearly afraid, so he puts his hands on hers, looks her in the eye and says, "One, two, three, lift!" They lift up the object and when it's about half a metre off the ground he tells her, "Now, you on your own." Very slowly he takes his hands away from hers, leaving her standing there, holding the slim, green cylinder in the air. Mikhail is the first to laugh. Then most of the others laugh too. "A rocket launcher!" Herr Lenzinger says, slapping his palm on the table. "It could have been," Laurenz says, looking as if he's on the verge of laughter too.

Jutta puts the object down, then turns and goes back to

her father. "Was it heavy?" he asks. "Not very," she says. He asks if she could have kept holding it for a long time and she says, yes, a really long time, as long as they would have had to hold up the hanged American to prevent him from dying. "Who would the people have had to hold up?" Grete asks. "The hanged American," Jutta says. "What's the child saying?" Laurenz asks. The vet gestures dismissively with his hand. That's a story in itself, he says, there's no need to go into it now. "Yes!" Jutta says. No, her father insists, maybe tomorrow.

"So what's really in there?" Antonia says, as acidly as only she can. Mikhail looks around circumspectly. "A picture," he says. Antonia says that's nonsense, pictures are flat, and Mikhail says, yes, pictures are flat when they're on walls, but if they're painted on paper or canvas you can remove them from their frames and roll them up. "What sort of a picture is it?" Antonia says. "One of mine," Mikhail says. "Are you a painter, then?" the farmer's wife asks. "I don't know," Mikhail says. Two homeless Danube Swabians, one with blast injuries, the other a man who paints pictures, but doesn't know if he's a painter, how remarkable, Laurenz says. "Maybe he's got blast injuries too," Antonia says – what sort of pictures does he paint? "Degenerate, I bet," Laurenz says, then bursts out laughing and promptly suffers a coughing fit. "That's your punishment," the farmer's wife says. Might it be possible to see the painting?

51

the vet says, he's very interested in paintings. No, Mikhail says, and when the vet asks why not, he says that the picture might get damaged if they roll it out here.

When Katharina and the farmer come to say that they've cleared part of the grain loft and laid down some straw sacks so he can have a sleep if he fancies, Mikhail has just devoured his third slice of bread and dripping. "You'll be sick," the vet says.

"He's going to eat us out of house and home," Antonia says. "He and Nelli."

The old man, whose name I still don't know, looks up. He's eaten a slice of bread and finished his glass of perry in small sips. Both his hands are shaking. He'd be very grateful if he might be permitted to lie down, he says. These are the only words he's spoken.

With the side of his hand Mikhail sweeps the bread-crumbs into a pile and dabs at it with his moistened fingertip. "Enough," he says. Frau Woitsch runs her fingers through her thin, yellow-white hair. She's not crying any-more.

Everybody stands up. The vet takes his daughter's hand. "It's just one night," he says to her. To the farmer he says, "I'll pay for that too," but the farmer gestures his rejec-tion of the offer. I don't know why, but at that moment I can't help thinking of St Lawrence on the hot coals and, at the same time, the feeling when Annemarie cosies up to my belly. I think of the stamp with the greyhound on the meadow, and that these people have eaten bread and dripping and are going to lie down, and that none of them has a clue how things will pan out, and all of a sudden I realise what I'd like to see now.

When I leave the parlour I glimpse out of the corner of my eye that it's half past three. This is the first time I've looked at the clock. Annemarie raises her eyebrows. "Go up," I say. "I'll be there in a minute."

Mikhail is the last to enter the hallway. His rolled-up picture is hanging by its strap over his shoulder. He's wearing black army boots that don't go with his filthy canvas clothes. When he notices me staring at them he says, "Too big." "Where is Templin really?" I ask, and he says it's in the district of Uckermark, north-east of Berlin. He asks me why I said that thing about Reșița, and I say sometimes you've got to act as if you've got everything under control. "What's your real name?" I say. "Mikhail," he says, that is his real name, Mikhail with two "i"s – in German people often fail to hear this.

"Mikhail what?"

"Levyokin," he says. "Mikhail Levyokin from Udranka."

Udranka is a village near Minsk, he tells me, and in case I'm interested, he learned German partly from his maternal grandmother who lived in Königsberg, but mostly in

53

Templin, where he did forced labour in a veneer factory after arriving as a prisoner-of-war in August 1941.

I'm standing there with what must be a fairly stupid expression on my face, for he asks what's wrong. "Nothing," I say. I don't tell him that I've never seen a Russian before.

He reaches out and taps my nose with his index finger. I hate that sort of thing normally. He smiles. "Here I'm a Danube Swabian," he says, "and Templin is near Reşiţa. Agreed?"

"Agreed," I say. "You've forgotten painter. A Danube Swabian painter." "Exactly," he says. "Suprematist."

The two of us go outside. He turns left. I ask him where he's going, and he says he's retiring to the hay. I ask why, and also how he knows where the hay is. He says he's spent long enough sharing a room with other people and doesn't need to do that anymore. He always knows where the hay is.

I sit in the grass beside the stunted blackthorn and gaze down at the town. The church towers, the town hall, and beyond these the fire, covering half of the horizon. I see red, yellow and black, and only then the night sky. I wait for a while, but no wagons explode. It's utterly silent, no engines, no sirens, not even any birds. I think of Frau Woitsch's yellow-white hair, the signal box on the outskirts of the station and the old man's shaking hands. Suddenly I wish the Russian would come and tap my nose again with his finger. Then it strikes me I have no idea what a Suprematist is – perhaps it's something like a spy after all.

For three days it rained cats and dogs, which left the surrounding fields under water and washed the tomato seedlings away. This wasn't, however, a major problem for the Madna airfield because, unlike the other airfields around Foggia, it was flood-proof. That morning some largish puddles were still sitting at the end of the runway, reflecting the pink sky. Otherwise the water had disappeared.

The runways at Lucera and Ramitelli had also declared themselves to all intents and purposes ready. The report from Lucera explained that a fuel tanker had got stuck on the access road, so there would be a delay of around forty-five minutes. But apart from this, they said, the B-17s were ready for take-off.

Shortly after six o'clock, Benjamin Shaffer, second lieutenant of the 52nd fighter group of the 5th squadron of the American Air Force left the barracks with eleven colleagues to board his Mustang. Alongside him were Simon McElroy, Matt Finley and Randy Shoemaker, his three best friends amongst the pilots of the Yellow Tails. A squadron of Red Tails was scheduled to arrive from Ramitelli. Twelve Red

Tail Tuskegees on one side, twelve Yellows on the other and, in-between, twenty Flying Fortresses and eight Liberators. This was the formation in which they would go about their work. Their targets were two railway junctions and the steelworks that bore the name of the Reichsmarschall. Linz. Apparently it was Hitler's favourite city, but so many things were said which nobody could ever verify.

Matt Finley made the sign of the cross over them all, and Randy Shoemaker said three times in succession that they should take care not to crash into an angel. This combination had now become a ritual before they climbed into their aircraft. McElroy muttered something about the pisspot of the Adriatic Sea starting to get on his nerves. He came from San Luis Obispo in California and if he stood on tiptoe he could see the waves of the Pacific crashing to the shore from the balcony of his bedroom. Benjamin Shaffer wondered briefly whether there was anything he missed about Akron, Ohio, the town he came from. Nothing sprung to mind.

"When you take off it looks as if you're pulling a string of pearls into the sky," Willie O'Shea, the airfield controller, used to say. "And when you return you look like a handful of bumblebees spat out by a tornado." As they climbed, Shaffer fancied he could actually feel the string of pearls. He could see Albert Ostrowski, the sullen farmer's son from Bakersfield, in front of him, he knew that Randy was behind him, and that Simon was behind Randy. He liked it that this order always stayed the same.

They quickly climbed to eight thousand feet, slotted into their final formation five hundred feet above the bombers and flew northwards across the Adriatic. A layer of cloud hung midway in the sky above the Veneto, which thickened as they approached the Friulian and Julian Alps, but then vanished fairly abruptly. The stretch between the lakes of Carinthia and the Alpine divide was totally clear, then beyond that was the odd insignificant accumulation of cloud.

Above the Ennstal they received the message that a squadron of German Messerschmitts was on its way from Graz to intercept them. This caused some alarm, but soon afterwards the message was retracted. Otherwise their flight was trouble-free.

After they reached the Danube at Ybbs and veered left, Randy Shoemaker radioed Shaffer to ask if he knew what was manufactured at the Hermann Göring works. Schaffer pondered this briefly, then said he didn't have a clue, but whatever was produced there, the buildings would definitely have very solid foundations. Shoemaker tried to imitate Göring by saying "Stuka" several times, which ended with him in a fit of laughter.

Later it was impossible to tell whether this was the precise point at which Benjamin Shaffer looked at the fuel gauge and realised it was time to jettison the drop tank. At any rate he was fully focused on working out where best to release the tank when he happened to glance ahead again. This may explain why, to begin with, he was only partially aware of the row of tiny white clouds possibly two miles away. *Like a string of pearls*, Willie O'Shea would say, and he also thought how astonishing it was that people so often fell back on the same similes.

At roughly the same time Isolde Kleinschmidt crossed the main square and entered the small hat shop, partly to stock the till, but also to get ready for an appointment. She could have left the change in her bag, for hardly any customers had come into the shop over the past few days. The last one had been the notoriously cranky town archivist, who had bought a pair of ear warmers with a fur trim. When Isolde pointed out that it was now the start of spring, he replied that his ears didn't care. The shop's penultimate customer had been a woman unfamiliar to her, in an elegant, coffee-coloured suit. In the end she'd taken a pair of beige leather gloves, as well as a double packet of white pocket squares. "For your husband?" Isolde asked, and the woman said, "No, for my sons – twins." Isolde also remembered that she hadn't dared ask the woman where she was from.

She strolled along the shelves. Knitted hats, caps, hats, headscarves. She could have listed the position of every item in her sleep. She stopped beside a broad-brimmed, anthracite man's fedora. *Her* hat. She would use it again. Some things just worked. Isolde went to the rear of the shop and entered the tiny, windowless storeroom, switched on the light, spread a white-linen cloth over the sorting table and carefully smoothed it with the palm of her hand. Then she stood there for a while, peering out into the salesroom and humming a few notes. Something about the melody wasn't right and so she stopped.

The chemist arrived at half past seven on the dot. She opened the door and locked it behind them straightaway. He removed the cap from his head, undid his belt and laid his long, grey S.A. coat on the chair beside the mirror. "Do we have to have the armband?" she said, pointing to his left arm. "Just be happy there aren't two of them," he said with a grin. "Can we?" No, she said, he'd promised her something else. "Promised?" he said. Yes, for her mother, she said, holding out her hand. He gave a resounding laugh.

"You're not talking about a new family tree, are you?"

She looked at him silently. He felt in the inner pocket of the coat he'd taken off and pulled out two little medicine tubes. "Prontosil, there you go," he said. "Three tablets per day. Now, can we . . .?" Isolde turned and made for the storeroom.

"You've got beautiful hair," the chemist said, unbuttoning his knee breeches. Isolde sat on the edge of the sorting table with the white cloth and looked at the thickset figure opposite her, the bald head and the lust on his face. "I know," she said, closing her eyes.

She saw before her the dark-grey fedora with its broad brim, saw herself take it from the shelf and turn it around a few times before placing it on her auburn plait. She saw herself look in the mirror, smile back at herself and finally she saw her torso and head, entirely separated from her lower half, float through the shop to the door, wearing the man's hat.

The shell penetrated the front third of the drop tank, entered the wing by the machine gun and exploded inside it. Benjamin Shaffer felt the impact, saw the white blaze to his right and heard the bang. Several thoughts came to mind simultaneously: that he could kiss goodbye to the idea that he'd always be capable of bringing his plane safely back to earth, even when it had been hit; that if he'd dropped the tanks earlier the shell would probably have passed straight through the wing and not exploded till afterwards; that Akron, Ohio, was a town that stank all year round of tyre rubber and bitumen, and all those who said you stopped smelling it after a few years weren't telling the truth; and, finally, that Randy Shoemaker had possibly been right the whole time when he warned about colliding with angels.

He was in a strangely calm mood when he radioed that he'd been hit, wrenched the aircraft to the left to exit the formation, cut his speed and undid the safety belt. After making sure that the strap of the pull cord was in its rightful place, below his left shoulder, he cut the engine, burst open the plexiglass canopy from the cockpit and climbed out. He didn't notice that he was the only one who'd been hit, nor that two Tuskegees peeled away from the formation, flew down in a double spiral, did several loops, but then failed to locate the flak which had stopped firing after a few salvos. Ultimately, he was also spared the sight of the burning wing tearing off his aeroplane a few hundred metres before it hit the ground.

Benjamin Joseph Shaffer, second lieutenant of the United States Army Air Forces, was found early in the morning beside his parachute in a meadow belonging to the municipality of Eisenreichdornach, around two kilometres to the east of the town, and taken into custody by the local police force. He was dazed after his jump and complained of a pain in his left elbow, but he was able to walk freely and without support. As his pistol had been confiscated and he appeared to present no danger, the chief gendarme Hans Redler instructed that he did not need to be manacled while he was marched into town. Only when the air-raid warning sounded as they reached the outskirts and had to find an underground shelter were handcuffs put on him.

It's hard to say exactly what turned the mood against

Shaffer. What is certain is that, amongst the people in that cellar near the hospital, there were some S.A. men who soon started claiming that the Americans' real goal was to flatten every town and city in the German Reich so that afterwards they could keep the surviving population as slaves. The Americans had always been good at destruction and enslavement, they said.

By the time the all-clear was given more than three hours later, two of Shaffer's incisors had been knocked out and he had a cut above his right eye. The fact that he was still alive was less down to Gendarme Redler's determination and rather thanks to a spontaneous idea that had come to him. When the people, men and women, began to physically attack Shaffer and the calls for a rope became ever louder, Redler told them – primarily to preserve some vestige of his authority, no doubt – not to worry, they would be allowed to hang the man in due course, but first he had to be shown to the chemist.

So the all-clear was given, and the most likely course of events was that they would have led Shaffer, covered in blood and with his hands tied behind his back, up Preinsbacher Strasse into town, and of course the fresh bomb damage would only have stoked the people's fury towards him even further. The gendarme would have had his hands full trying to prevent the American from being stoned to death before they reached the main square. In the end all Redler would have said was, "You can hang him anyway."

The chemist would have been standing outside his shop, arms crossed, watching the crowd with perceptible pleasure. He would have gone up to the American, reached for his neck and pulled out his dog tag. He would have glanced at it, then grinned and asked the crowd, "What do we do with enemies of the Volk?" He would have dismissed the argument from S.A. squad leader Asbeck, also present, that these people were always handy for things such as finding unexploded ordnance.

The crowd would have gathered under a lantern at the north-western end of the square and Gendarme Redler would have stood beside the chemist, looking relaxed and free of responsibility. Afterwards it would have been irrelevant whether the rope was actually fetched from the nearby ropemaker in Ardagger Strasse, or where the wooden ladder came from that they used.

The American would have resisted, of course, but at the chemist's prompting a few strong volunteers would have come forward at once. They would have lifted up the man, kept him sufficiently still, and dropped him at the right moment.

That was the most likely course of events.

Later Isolde Kleinschmidt seldom talked about how

she'd stepped outside the shop because of the noise, how she initially thought there was something wrong with the lantern and then she heard the chemist shouting. It was a very mixed crowd, with women and children present too, two female teachers from the primary school, the municipal architect and his son, old Frau Schwabl, who'd felt persecuted even before the war. At this point the American was sitting on the ground. She only noticed him, she said, when the chemist beckoned her over. "Shall I show you something?" he asked with a grin. She merely shrugged, at which he grabbed the man by the coat, pulled him up and held his dog tag under her nose. "Read!" the chemist ordered.

So long as she lived, Isolde said, she would never forget the man's dark-brown eyes, and so long as she lived, she would know by heart what she read out that day: "Benjamin J. Shaffer, 52071193, T43–44, AB, H." Did she know what T43–44 meant? the chemist asked, and when she shook her head, he howled and slapped the man on the shoulder. "It means he's been vaccinated against tetanus!" he barked, and AB was his blood group. He may be an enemy of the Volk, but he had a rare blood group.

Finally, she said, he pointed to the H, grinned once more and asked her if she knew what that meant. At that moment she pictured in her mind the broad-brimmed fedora, herself floating through the shop, and a ridiculous bald man in the back room, toiling away at the lower body of a woman. Yes, she said, she knew precisely what it meant.

Right after that she bent down to his ear and said she didn't care about the consequences, she was going to tell people everything, she was going to say it loud and clear. She was going to say what H meant and who she was and what the chemist did with her. Everybody in this square was going to hear it, the municipal architect, the S.A. and his wife. She herself would be very relieved.

With an expression of surprise he turned around, she said, and gave the gendarme a sign. "Who are the enemies of the Volk?" he'd called out to the crowd. "Are we such barbarians too?" Without waiting for the crowd's reaction he said straightaway that the man should be taken to the camp and be sent out to look for unexploded ordnance.

March 29th, 1945

Antonia is flying. She gives the impression of skipping in small arcs through the air and only ever touching the ground very briefly. There's a shining fury on her face, which instantly makes you want to hug her, even though you know she'll want to wallop you. She's after Mikhail, even a blind man could see that. She watches him, she follows him wherever he goes, and if anyone else shows an interest in him she turns into a guard dog on the spot. She even reserves the right to talk badly of him. "You're a crank and you're eating us out of house and home," she tells him, and from her expression you can see that she's being serious. He just laughs. When I tell her all these things she says I should keep my mouth shut, I'm a liar and a foundling who suffered blast injuries, and I don't even know what my real name is. She's had Katharina redo her plait. I don't tell her that I've noticed.

The weather is still lovely and so warm that I can go around in a house dress. The coltsfoot is still in flower, the dandelions are just starting and the first buds on the forsythia are opening. The yellow period is beginning, Grete says, which comes as a surprise as she never says things like this. The farmer says the potatoes don't care whether it's wartime or not, they need to go into the ground so long as it's reasonably dry.

Laurenz has parked the cart on the edge of the field and is unharnessing the horse. Using a long hemp rope that he ties with a knot to the bit ring, he tethers the animal so it can graze in relative freedom. When he sees us approaching he stops. "I've got something for you at home," he tells Mikhail. "What?" Mikhail asks. "Paper," he says.

"What sort of paper?"

"No idea," Laurenz says. "Two hundred plain sheets." "I have to see it," Mikhail says. "You don't need to see anything, you need to sow potatoes," Antonia says, planting herself in front of him. Mikhail hesitates, smiles and salutes.

The paper is thicker than writing paper, a touch coarse and light grey rather than white, Laurenz says. Herr Streit, the stationer, said it ought to be ideal for his purposes. Apparently it's remaindered stock from a paper mill in the Waldviertel. That sort of paper isn't being manufactured at the moment. "Who on earth needs light-grey paper?" Antonia says. Mikhail says nothing.

Laurenz and the farmer's wife stay on the cart, cutting the seed potatoes in half. I don't ask why they're doing that. Some things are just right. We walk side by side, laying the cut potatoes in the furrows the farmer ploughed this morning. There are six of us and we take turns to help ourselves from a basket in pairs: Antonia and Mikhail, Roswitha and I, Herr and Frau Lenzinger. The house in which the omnibus driver and his wife live has suffered blast damage from the bomb that fell on the neighbouring property. The farmer and his wife have said they can stay for a few weeks if they help on the farm.

The freshly ploughed earth has a funny smell to it. I can't help imagining an underground realm populated by moles and dormice, all of them quite intelligent and making fun of people. I have no idea why such things fill my head.

Mikhail is going along the row to the right of me and Antonia further away to the right. After a while I ask him what he's going to draw on the paper. He says he doesn't know, it depends on the inspiration. "Maybe moles and mice?" I say. Not moles, he says, and I say, but moles are like royal creatures. Antonia asks why I'm talking about moles and mice, normally I witter on about geography and martyrs. I think about this briefly, then say, "Alright then, why not martyrs?" Mikhail says he's never drawn martyrs either and doesn't know whether he'd be able to, even if he wasn't a Suprematist.

"Male or female?" I say. "Doesn't matter," he says. "Three men, three women?" I say. "If you like," he says.

Not Stephen, I say, he's too boring. Stoning, that's just like being killed normally.

Florian, on the other hand, his shoulder blade is broken with a sharp instrument, then they tie a millstone around his neck and chuck him into the River Enns.

Or Sebastian. First they shoot arrows at him, and when he survives they beat him to death with wooden clubs.

"But my favourite is still Bartholomew," I say. "Why?" Mikhail says. "They remove his skin with a flaying knife," I say. "What's a flaying knife?" Antonia says. "The knacker's knife," I say.

"And what's a knacker?"

"Someone who strips the skin off animals."

"Dead animals?" Roswitha says. She hasn't said anything until now. "I hope so!" Antonia says.

"What about the women?" Mikhail says. They're even lovelier, I say.

Agatha, for example, I say. Her breasts are cut off, then she's roasted over hot coals until she dies.

Frau Lenzinger stands up straight. "Is that really necessary?" she asks. I say I'm not the person to ask that question, and she says she means, do I have to tell such gruesome stories? "He's an artist," I say, and then I say that there are only two more to go anyway. "Then don't exaggerate," she says. I haven't exaggerated one bit, but I don't say this.

Margarete, I say. They let a dragon into her cell, they burn her armpits with torches and then there are two versions. In the first they drown her in a tub of water, in the other she's tossed into boiling oil. "I'd prefer the oil," Antonia says. "Why?" I ask. "Just because," she says.

But my favourite is Lucy, I say. They gouge the eyes out of her head. "Please stop," Roswitha says. She's so pale it looks as if she might faint at any moment. "I told you so!" Frau Lenzinger looks at me reproachfully, puts an arm around Roswitha and walks her to the cart.

"I didn't exaggerate anything," I say when the two have gone. Antonia shrugs. "She's strange," I say. Roswitha is pale with freckles, she doesn't eat much and rarely says a word. She'll turn twelve at the end of April, that's the only thing I know about her. I've no idea what goes on inside her head.

He would be interested in the faces, Mikhail says, after we've been sowing in silence for a while. He could imagine drawing the faces of those martyrs. "With no skin and no eyes?" Antonia says. Yes, he says, or under water or just at the moment they're put on hot coals.

"Do you have a family?" I ask him. He looks at me in astonishment.

"In Udranka, near Minsk – do you still have family there?"

He gives the impression of really having to think this over. "I don't know," he says eventually.

On the way home the farmer's wife takes me aside and says she knows she told me all those martyr stories, but I mustn't abuse them. I look up ahead at the cart, where Roswitha is sitting. She's allowed to ride on it because she almost fainted. I think abuse is a terrible word and say, yes, I understand.

We see a pair of hawks circling above the spruce trees and a hamster scurrying across the meadow. I reckon hamsters aren't royal creatures.

I think of the fact that Mikhail has used almost half the hay for the billet he's made himself, and that Laurenz has said it doesn't matter because the cattle will be going out to pasture soon. I think of the fact that the farmer's wife has washed his canvas clothes and that just now he's wearing Leo's things: a blue-and-white striped shirt, which fits him, and green corduroy trousers that are three centimetres too short. I think of the faces he talked about and of Leo's face, a face I don't know, not even from a photograph. In the end it occurs to me that I've forgotten to ask Mikhail which colours he's going to use on the light-grey paper.

On the slope up from the ditch to the farm, the farmer comes to meet us and tells us to stay where we are. He's out of breath. It's only the Wehrmacht – that's the first thing he says. Then he says we mustn't be shocked to see a military truck in the yard, it arrived with three soldiers: two corporals and a lieutenant. Judging by the accents, he says, one of the corporals is from Bavaria, while the other two soldiers are from northern Germany. He's offered them perry and shown them into the parlour. "Don't worry," he says, "they're not S.S." Mikhail's face is ashen. "Who am I?" he asks. "Mikhail Levyokin, a Danube Swabian from Templin near Reşiţa," I say. Everyone nods.

"Where are my papers?" he asks.

"The Russians have got them," I say.

"What about my family?"

"What would be your preference?"

"Dead, unfortunately," he says. Everyone nods once more.

The two corporals leap to their feet when we enter the parlour. The lieutenant gets up slowly. "Heil Hitler!" he says. He's slim, of medium height, and he wears nickel spectacles. His head is narrow, like a bird's. It's impossible to tell whether his hair is blond or white. When he speaks, from time to time he pauses between words, as if thinking. "We don't intend to" – pause – "take advantage of" – pause – "your hospitality" – pause – "for very long." This is how he speaks, and he says "my good lady" to the farmer's wife. "My good lady, we would very much appreciate a bite to eat." To the farmer he simply says "farmer". He says that the Second Army, to which they belong, is regrouping unit by unit so they can close in for the decisive counterattack.

I kick Antonia, who's standing beside me, for I sense she wants to say that we've heard Vienna's practically in the hands of the Russians, and on the other side the Americans are already in Upper Austria. She gives me a furious look and keeps her mouth shut.

The lieutenant tells us his name is Bernd Gollwitz and he comes from Aurich in Lower Saxony. It crosses my mind that there are some people whose name you don't want to know, such as those who say "unit by unit".

The lieutenant also says he's asking the farmer to free up the cart shed for their truck, in fact to empty it completely to give them space to unload their equipment too. Then he says he feels sure that the brave soldiers of the German Wehrmacht will be given a decent place to sleep, and finally that he will have to confiscate the wireless temporarily, for security reasons.

When the three of them are sitting at the table, eating smoked ham, bread and pickled beetroot, he says he's looking forward to the wonderful roast he and his men will enjoy tomorrow. The farmer's wife looks at him, says nothing and vanishes into the kitchen.

"I'm going to sleep in the hay," Antonia hisses to me as we go outside. "Me too," I say, "and Roswitha and Annemarie as well." "If you insist," she says. Antonia usually shares a double bed with Roswitha in the upstairs girls' room, while I share a narrower one in the maid's room. So that works out well for the soldiers.

We sort out the billets. The corporal with the Bavarian accent will have to sleep on the left, on Roswitha's side. "Because he's fat?" I ask. She shakes her head. "Because he sweats?" I ask. No, she says, not that either. Suddenly I get it. "Because he's so stupid," I say. Yes, Antonia beams, you can tell everything about some people even before they open their mouths. She feels that such stupidity could seep into her bed and she'd never be able to get rid of it again.

The farmer, Mikhail and Herr Lenzinger empty the cart shed. They take out the haycarts, large and small, the double axle one with the rubber wheels, the slurry barrel, the hay tedder and the two ploughs, and put them beneath the pear trees. Finally Mikhail sweeps the floor with a giant broom. "Isn't that a little excessive?" Herr Lenzinger says. You never know, Mikhail says, some people like it to be clean. He's still holding the broom when he turns to Laurenz and asks whether it would be possible to see the paper now. Laurenz nods. "I'll go and get it," he says. "And a pencil," Antonia calls after him.

A while later Mikhail is standing at the end of the large haycart, a sheet of light-grey drawing paper on the load bed in front of him, and beside the paper a slim, lime-green box. Everyone is standing around him, Antonia is especially close, and Laurenz is telling them how when he finished school he was given this box of pastels by his art teacher, who said they were going to a good home. Then he entered the seminary and didn't draw a single picture for the whole two years he was there.

"What are pastels?" Antonia asks, but nobody gives her an answer.

Herr Lenzinger says that the Way of the Cross in the parish church is beautifully painted, and the farmer says that, if he remembers correctly, he's always wanted a picture of the farm.

I think about the fact that Mikhail said he would be interested in martyrs' faces, without skin and under water and at that instant when they're placed on hot coals. I realise I didn't tell him how Lucy dies after her eyes are gouged out: by being stabbed in the neck.

Mikhail stands there, takes one pastel after another out of the box and lines them up side by side. "None have been used," Laurenz says. "All as good as new." Then he leans in to Mikhail and says softly, "Do you know what I'd like you to draw for me? A picture of Hitler." The omnibus driver looks around in horror. Laurenz laughs and has a coughing fit. If the farmer's wife were here, she would say, "That's your punishment."

Suddenly Mikhail picks up one of the pastels and draws a line right across the paper towards the top. It's purple.

"That's good," he says. "Victory over the sun."

Laurenz says that all artists are a bit crazy, otherwise they wouldn't be artists in the first place. Then he has another coughing fit.

If you concentrate you can peer into the night through the gaps between the boards of the barn. I like this – it's dark, but not completely black. Annemarie is quivering next to me. To begin with she fidgeted and kicked me like she usually does in bed, but then she was still. Now she feels like an animal having strange little shivering fits. Roswitha is lying on her back, breathing peacefully. I think of how some people faint and some almost do; sometimes it's caused by gouged-out eyes, and sometimes by the fact that someone wants to adopt you.

No sooner had Antonia lain down than she picked up her sheet and blanket and crept over to the other side of the hayloft, where Mikhail is. She did this very quietly, then couldn't stifle a sneeze and the two of them laughed. Now they're doing things – I don't care what. From time to time they talk. I hear "cover", "don't know", "nice here", "war" and other words. I picture Antonia's plait and her face when she recites a poem that ends with "You will not find them". Afterwards I gaze up at the darkness beneath the crest of the roof. I notice tears welling in my eyes. I don't wipe them away because of the hay dust. I think of how I'm lying here, crying between two sleeping girls, and of how sometimes everything in life is fine, and sometimes you wish it would all come to an end.

At some point in the middle of the night I wake up. The martens are scurrying around on the roof. Judging by the noise there must be at least two of them. Their claws sound like nails on metal, and occasionally I hear them hiss. Laurenz says that martens are out-and-out hunters and terrifically elegant. I still don't like them. Not because they empty birds' nests or because they broke into the rabbit hutch, leaving only one of the four baby rabbits alive, but because they're devious and mean. No amount of elegance can make up for that.

I think I dreamed of the railway, of a station so enormous that one could get lost in it, and of a city I didn't know. It had several bridges and nothing but white, yellow and orange houses. It could have been Reşiţa.

Annemarie is still asleep. During the night she buried herself deep in the covers and I can barely see her now. Roswitha is standing beside our billet, having neatly folded her nightwear and put it in a pile. Mikhail slips on his shirt, feels in the hay behind him, pulls out a few sheets of paper and the box of pastels, and says he has to go and draw. "Where's Antonia?" I ask. "She just went down," Mikhail says.

I run after Antonia and catch up with her beneath the pear trees by the double axle cart with the rubber wheels. We wander to the house together. Halfway between the cart shed and the front door we meet the slimmer of the two corporals. He's got red hair, but this is almost impossible to see when he's wearing his helmet. Antonia makes a bee-line for him, seemingly unconcerned by the assault rifle hanging across his shoulder. "How did you sleep?" she says. He takes a step back and looks shocked. "Well, thank you," he stammers, "although not quite enough. Why do you ask?" "Why not enough?" Antonia asks. He had sentry duty for the first half of the night, he says, and when Antonia asks why sentry duty, he says because those were his orders. "You slept in my bed," she says. For a while it seems as if he can't think of anything to say. Then he says, "I'm sorry about that."

The lieutenant is sitting at the table, a jug of milk and a glass in front of him. The farmer's wife is standing in the middle of the parlour, trembling, the farmer a couple of paces behind her, a few centimetres from the wall. "When I said *a roast*, I meant a roast!" the lieutenant says. "It's Good Friday," the farmer's wife says. Good Friday, Easter Saturday, Easter Sunday, he couldn't care less, the lieutenant says. If he says he wants a roast for himself and his men then it would be best for all concerned if he gets that roast.

With white cabbage and dumplings and lovely crackling, that's what he's been imagining, just like normal. "It's Good Friday here . . ." the farmer says. What does he mean, "here"? the lieutenant interrupts. The farmer doesn't respond to this. "Dumplings," Antonia says quietly. I elbow her in the side.

Besides, we don't have enough meat, the farmer's wife says. These are difficult times and nobody imagines they'll need meat on Good Friday. The lieutenant takes a sip from the glass. "Fetch me Schwertfeger," he says. Who? the farmer asks, and the lieutenant says, Schwertfeger, the Bavarian. "He did the second sentry duty and now he's asleep," he says. "Wake him." Antonia turns and leaves.

I look at the lieutenant's slim hands and picture this man drinking a glass of milk every day back home, then reading the paper, and how the family has to be completely quiet on a Sunday while he takes his afternoon nap. I imagine Aurich with a main street, a town hall that looks like a small castle, and all manner of houses surrounded by trees and shrubs. Finally I imagine there to be a place in Aurich where hot-air balloons take off and land, a large square with benches around the edge where one can sit and watch. The lieutenant puts on a brown-leather aviator hat and goggles, climbs into the basket of his balloon and waves goodbye. Sometimes I have to imagine such things, I can't help it.

When Antonia returns she is pale. The fat corporal is

carrying the assault rifle, as the red-headed one did earlier. As he enters the parlour he salutes. The lieutenant asks him whether he noticed anything suspicious on his patrols, and the corporal says no. The lieutenant asks whether he inspected the agricultural buildings too, and the corporal says yes, of course. Then the lieutenant asks what he saw in the animal sheds, for example. "Nothing suspicious," the corporal replies. "What, then?" the lieutenant asks. What does he mean? the corporal says, and the lieutenant replies, just what he said – what did he see in the animal sheds? "Animals," the corporal says eventually. "Cattle, pigs, horses." "Did you count them?" the lieutenant asks. The fat corporal turns red. No, he says, he did not, but there were two horses, he's sure of that. "And how many pigs?" the lieutenant asks. Two pigs as well, the corporal says, possibly three, but he couldn't be certain.

The lieutenant places his hands flat on the table and looks at the farmer and his wife in turn. The wife stands there, saying nothing. The farmer shakes his head. No, he says, he can't ask him to do that, not on Good Friday. The lieutenant waits a while, then he smiles and says, "You don't have to." He signals to the corporal and says, "Go and choose one for us."

Laurenz is outside with the horses and the sower to broadcast the summer barley. We fetch him from the field. After we tell him everything he breathes rapidly and doesn't say anything. "I'm going to kill him," Antonia says on the way home. "Who?" I say.

"The Bavarian."

"Because of the sow?"

No, she says, because he slept in her bed and not Roswitha's. When she went into the bedroom she saw him splayed out before her and knew instantly that his stupidity had already leached into the innermost layers of her bed. She was worried it was completely contaminated and now there was nothing left but to burn it. I think of how Antonia crept over to Mikhail last night, how she sneezed and how the two of them said all sorts of words, like "nice here" or "war". Then I think of how Schwertfeger is a peculiar name, but I say nothing. "Stop laughing so stupidly!" she hisses.

When we get back to the farmhouse, everything is as it usually is after sticking a pig. The sow is lying in a wooden tub in the narrow room between the pigshed and stable. The farmer is pouring boiling water over it and Grete and Katharina are scraping the bristles from its skin. They only just managed to bleed the pig, the farmer says. Shoot first and think later, so typical of people like that. I look around. Antonia doesn't appear to have heard.

After scalding the pig they tie the hind legs to a yoke with an iron ring on each side and hoist it up to the ceiling with the help of a well wheel. Laurenz and the farmer slice down the length of the pig and remove the innards. Then they chop its head off. There is a crash as the skull falls to the floor. I don't like to look. I imagine two dark holes in the head, that's enough for me.

It's half past three when the roast is finally ready. It took some time to joint the sow, and then the kitchen oven had to be heated to the right temperature. The rest was as usual – cabbage, dumplings, everything. While shredding the cabbage the farmer's wife looked up just once and said she knew for sure that she would pay in Purgatory for what she was doing here. Then she went on shredding the cabbage, as if everything were perfectly normal, like on any Sunday morning. The lieutenant put his head round the kitchen door several times, saying on each occasion, "Good things take time."

Annemarie has been sitting on the bench by the stove for more than an hour, commenting how wonderfully it smells of garlic and caraway. I think so too, although I get a bad conscience because I used to feed that pig from time to time, and it was one of those piglets that the farmer's wife and Grete hand-reared with the bottle. Sometimes mothers reject their offspring; apparently it's the same with all creatures. I really couldn't care less about Good Friday and Purgatory, but I keep this to myself.

The lieutenant gets up, taps on the jug with his knife and

asks if everyone is present. Antonia is missing, the farmer's wife says, and the lieutenant asks where she is. "At prayer," the farmer's wife says, "so that at least one of us is." "And the tall lad?" he asks. Which tall lad, the farmer's wife says, and the lieutenant says, the young man who says he's a Danube Swabian. "He's outside, drawing," I say. Once again the lieutenant lays his palms flat on the table. It would be better for the Danube Swabian if he came in and ate with us, he says, we should pass that message on to him.

Mikhail is standing at the end of the haycart drawing, just as before. Antonia is leaning against the side of the cart, watching him. There are several pictures on the load bed. When he notices me trying to peer over his shoulder he quickly flips over the picture he's in the middle of drawing. They both laugh. Spying is forbidden, he says, you're only allowed to see finished pictures. "What are you drawing?" I ask. "A square," he says, laughing again. I can see colour all over his hands, red, black, white and yellow, they look feral. I glance at the other drawings. "What's that supposed to be?" I ask. "A house," Mikhail says, "and a castle." "And an aeroplane, a dark pond, a cow and a jumping jack," Antonia says. I see squares, rectangles, crescents, ellipses and no dark pond. All of a sudden I can't help thinking of when I looked down at the town in the darkness, at the roofs, the church towers and the burning oil train. I tell Mikhail that the lieutenant doesn't trust him and he says he thought that right away. "Reșiţa is a beautiful city," I say, "it only has white, yellow and orange houses." He raises his eyebrows and acts as if he's amazed. I couldn't think of anything better to say.

"Heil Hitler!" the lieutenant says when we enter the parlour. "Heil Hitler!" Mikhail returns the greeting. The lieutenant asks what sorts of pictures he's been drawing all day long, and Mikhail replies, a castle, a dark pond and an aeroplane. What sort of aeroplane? the lieutenant asks. A British Lancaster over Berlin, Mikhail replies, and when the lieutenant looks surprised he says, a Lancaster about to crash. The red-headed corporal laughs loudly, which earns him a reproachful look from the lieutenant. "We'll take a look at that afterwards," he says.

Each of us is invited to say something about ourselves. This is the only way a meal can be entertaining, the lieutenant says. The red-headed corporal, whose name is Friedrich, says that in Emsland, where he comes from, there are windmills and peat digging, and the cows, which are either black or black and white, are the best dairy cattle in the world. His father has a small brick factory and his elder sister was born with a mildly crippled arm, but she managed to become a lawyer's assistant nonetheless. When the war is won he's going to take over the business himself and make good money as the country is rebuilt. "What do people need when everything's been destroyed? Bricks!" he says. He shovels in huge mouthfuls of food. His nervousness and anxious, wide eyes give the impression he's worried that the brick factory and his sister with the crippled arm might no longer exist. Herr Lenzinger notices this and puts a hand on his arm. Then he tells a few of his omnibus driver's tales. Since he's been staying with us we've heard them all several times, but that doesn't matter. For example, the story of the Benedictine padre who had a minor stroke during a journey and then no longer knew which monastery he belonged to. Or the story of the elderly lady who fell asleep in the back row, was forgotten and then the following morning knocked against the glass, shouting "Help!" even though he was already at her side. Or the story of the wages clerk who had been driven mad by the war, and one morning got aboard the omnibus and started playing with a hand grenade among the other passengers.

"Well, at least it didn't explode," the lieutenant says. No, not in the bus, that was indeed fortunate.

"How about you?" the lieutenant says, turning abruptly to Antonia. She stares at her plate and doesn't answer. What about her? the farmer's wife says. Antonia is their middle child, that's to say the fourth if you include their son. "Your son?" the lieutenant asks. Yes, the farmer's wife says, their son, the second eldest. "Where is he?" the lieutenant asks, and the farmer's wife says the last letter

86

they had was from Aachen, but that was ages ago. I look over at Laurenz. He's put some cabbage onto his fork and is staring into the distance.

"How were your prayers?" the lieutenant asks. Antonia lifts her head and looks at him directly. Quiet, she says, as ever on Good Friday. No church bells or music, and the altar boys had strange wooden rattles instead of their usual hand bells. In his sermon the priest said the war would soon be over, and then it was especially quiet, she says.

The farmer's wife presses her fingers to her eyes. The lieutenant puts his cutlery to one side. Yes, that's correct, he says, the war will soon be over. The German Volk will rise up and all those who would have liked to see things turn out differently will grovel before us. Then he really gets going. He starts talking louder, but not shouting, and when he's finished the red-headed corporal from Emsland is as white in the face as Roswitha was yesterday.

By the end, Herr Lenzinger and Corporal Schwertfeger have eaten the most, that's to say three pieces of meat and two dumplings, followed by Mikhail – two pieces of meat and two dumplings – then the lieutenant and Katharina, both of whom have eaten two pieces of meat and one and a half dumplings. The farmer's wife, Grete and Antonia haven't eaten any meat and Laurenz only a little, although he said earlier that he wasn't hungry. I feel a bit silly, but sometimes counting things helps.

As the table is being cleared, the lieutenant tells stories from East Frisia, about spring tides and mudflats and what it's like around Aurich when the rhododendrons flower in May. When he finishes he waves Mikhail over, saying there's something else he wants to ask him about Templin.

The Story of the Suprematist
Who Wasn't Shot

The day when Jakob Leithner was a hero began with his wife colouring eggs. Although she had already collected a number the previous week, she nonetheless went into the chicken shed after feeding and milking the cows, and removed all the eggs from the nests. This was usually the girls' job, but Easter Saturday was always an exception. In the end she counted sixty eggs, roughly as many as in past years. This reassured her. She took the eggs into the kitchen, put a large pot of water on the stove and added a few dashes of vinegar. Then she went into the vegetable cellar, fetched a basketful of onions, peeled them, and dropped the dry skins into the water. She hadn't been able to find red egg colouring anywhere this year, not at the paint shop, nor even at Hans Schellander's chemist's, where she usually bought these things.

Half an hour later there were two flat straw baskets full of hard-boiled eggs on the kitchen table, all of them dyed beautifully evenly, from a golden ochre to a chestnut brown, depending on how long they had sat in the onion-peel liquor. She greased them with bacon rind and then polished them till they shone. Half of the eggs would be taken along to the church on Easter night to be blessed, and the others would be given away unblessed. The farmer's wife was content and, if anyone had been with her at that moment, she would likely have said that this was one of those occasions when she felt really wealthy.

To begin with Barbara Leithner wasn't unsettled by the noises coming from the room next door. She intuitively thought it was the children who might have got up early, which was entirely understandable given the unusual sleeping arrangements over the past few nights. Only when the soldier, whose name she had learned yesterday was Corporal Schwertfeger, appeared in the doorway and said that the lieutenant wanted a jug of milk and a few glasses did she realise she was mistaken. She went to the window, poured milk from the enamel pitcher into the jug and gave it to the soldier. "Is that strictly necessary?" she asked, pointing at the assault rifle over his shoulder. Schwertfeger gave a somewhat embarrassed shrug. He feared it was, yes, he said.

When, a few moments later, Barbara came into the parlour with three glasses, the first thing that caught her attention was the chair in the middle of the room, as if it had been left there by mistake. She walked over to it. "Leave it!" the lieutenant said. Bernd Gollwitz, lieutenant of the Second Panzer Army of the German Wehrmacht, was sitting at the table, eyeing the chair over the rims of his spectacles. Clearly he was trying to work out the correct distance. The farmer's wife put down the glasses. "What's this about?" she asked. "I don't wish to be impolite, but it's none of your business, my good lady," he said, and she almost retorted that she harboured her doubts as to whether she really was a good lady.

"Where is he?" the lieutenant asked. "Behind the cart shed," Schwertfeger replied. "Friedrich says he's drawing again. He started at dawn." "Bring him here," the lieutenant said. Then he motioned to the farmer's wife to leave the room.

When the two corporals suddenly appeared beside the hay-cart and the fat one asked him to follow them into the house, Mikhail Levyokin gave the impression that he was expecting something like this. Levyokin gathered his drawings into a pile and put the pastels back into the box. "Shall I wash my hands?" he said, holding up his palms for the two corporals to see. The red-headed one said he didn't think that would be necessary.

When they entered the parlour, the lieutenant said, "Sit down!" and pointed to the chair in the middle of the room. Levyokin looked around. "What's happening?" he asked. "We're going to have a conversation," the lieutenant said.

But we already did that yesterday evening, Levyokin said.

Yesterday evening the conversation was about private matters, the lieutenant said. This was different. So would he be so kind as to . . .

Levyokin put the small pile of drawings on the floor and sat down. Corporal Schwertfeger was instructed to stand by the door, while the redhead was placed at the head of the table with a sheet of paper and a pen.

"What is your name, sir?" the lieutenant asked. Again Levyokin looked surprised. "Why the formality?" he asked. "As I said," the lieutenant replied, "this is no longer a private discussion, so if you would be so kind . . ."

"Mikhail Yegorovich Levyokin."

"Born?"

"November the fourth, nineteen hundred and nineteen."

So young, the lieutenant said. Was Levyokin a Danube Swabian name? "No," Levyokin said.

"What, then?"

"Russian."

Aha, the lieutenant said, so how had he come up with this Danube Swabian story? But he'd told him everything yesterday, Levyokin replied. Gollwitz sprang to his feet and slapped his palm on the tabletop. "Yesterday was a private conversation!" he barked. Levyokin closed his eyes for a moment. Then he said that the girl had come up with the idea and it had appealed to him. The girl, Nelli, she was from a Danube Swabian family whose house had been bombed and she herself had suffered an injury, but at least she had papers, unlike him.

The girl, who to his knowledge came from Reşiţa, the lieutenant said, from Reşiţa in the Banat, close to Timişoara and even closer to Templin. Levyokin shook his head.

What then?

But he'd already . . .

"Then tell me again!" the lieutenant yelled.

"The whole story?" Levyokin asked, and the lieutenant said, yes, the whole story.

He, Mikhail Yegorovich Levyokin, an art student originally from the village of Udranka near Minsk, the young man said, joined the Soviet Army in April 1941 and was taken prisoner by the Germans as a private of the 47th Rifle Corps at the Battle of Białystok on June 30th, 1941. Before being taken prisoner he'd emptied at most two magazines of his assault rifle and he was fairly certain he hadn't hit anyone, but nobody was interested in this.

As a prisoner he was first taken, along with thousands of others, to P.O.W. camp 352 in Masyukovchina. There his life was saved by a German captain by the name of Lippert. To this day he couldn't say what the man found interesting about him, perhaps it was just his knowledge of German; at any rate, Lippert helped him to escape that hell-hole in August 1941, after six weeks, and secure a job as a foreign slave worker in the Drexler & Spatt veneer factory in Templin. He made several enquiries about Captain Lippert subsequently, but was unable to garner any information about the man, neither how he was best contactable, nor whether he had any connection to Drexler & Spatt.

To begin with he worked on the steaming vats, then in cutting and packaging, and finally on the peeling machines, which was the most difficult task of all and the one with the highest level of responsibility. He was perfectly happy working for the company for three and a half years – food, lodging, everything was fine – and what happened had nothing to do with the conditions there. In truth nobody was surprised that orders in the firm's core business had dried up – who buys expensive furniture when the world is falling to pieces? – and they were well prepared to divert to subsidiary activities, such as transport services.

On the morning of February 27th they were given the task of collecting some containers from Carinhall in Schorf-heide forest, taking them to Oranienburg station where they would load them onto a waiting goods wagon. He drove there with his foreman, Joachim, in one of the three-tonne Opels. Joachim said he'd always wanted to see how the Reichsmarschall lived. Levyokin did not care for such things himself, Göring and his Carinhall, and basically they saw nothing except for stone walls and the barred windows of the gatehouse. For the items they were to transport were already at the gate. Two medium-sized wooden containers, sealed on all sides, and a crate that was open at the top – he had a clear recollection of the cargo, likewise of the driver of the forklift, who had taken an age to deposit the boxes on the load bed. He immediately noticed that the address on the labels read MAUTERNDORF / SALZBURG. He also saw that the oilcloth cover had come away from the slim package in the crate, revealing a broad, golden picture frame.

Maybe one could say it was a sort of contagion or a minor fit of obsession, but at any rate the moment they arrived at Oranienburg he couldn't help himself, he insisted on being shut into the goods wagon along with the boxes.

At this point Lieutenant Gollwitz interrupted Levyokin's story and told him to spare them this sentimental nonsense – the artist who becomes mesmerised by mere contact with a painting – nobody would believe a word of it. Gollwitz said he was more interested in how much hush money he'd paid his foreman, for this Joachim character would also have to be made accountable for his actions. Moreover, what had Levyokin done with the items in the containers? Destroyed them? Sabotaged them? Sold them? "Looked at them," Levyokin said. It was a long journey and light enough, for the wagon had a skylight, so he lifted the objects out of the crate and removed them from their packaging. "And?" the lieutenant asked. "Yellow cows, distorted faces and the occasional blue sun," Levyokin said, much of it not his sort of thing, but there was no doubt as to its quality.

For a moment the lieutenant sat there quietly, then slowly he rose from his chair, supported himself on the tabletop and bent forwards. He couldn't tell for sure whether this was just a barefaced lie or an attempt to denigrate the Reichsmarschall's taste in art. Either way it amounted to sheer infamy, which of course should come as no surprise from a liar, traitor and cowardly deserter. On the other hand, now was perhaps a good time. Pointing to the pile on the floor, he said, "Show us one of your scribbles."

Levyokin bent down, picked up the sheets of paper and set them side by side on the table. "What's that supposed to be, then?" the lieutenant asked. Suprematism, Levyokin replied.

Suprematism. He understood.

The art of pure form, detached from the subject, from nature and from mankind.

Who did he get this nonsense from? the lieutenant asked. He couldn't see any pure form, just a distorted square, six infantile-looking rectangles and a clumsy attempt at a diamond. Levyokin didn't reply. "Well?" the lieutenant asked again. No matter, Levyokin said, the lieutenant didn't know these people. Absolutely right, the lieutenant said, and nor did he have any interest in getting to know them.

"Is that all?" he asked. Levyokin nodded. "The old man's got something too," Schwertfeger said from beside the door. "Which old man?" the lieutenant asked. The farmer's brother, Schwertfeger replied, he'd seen a few of these pieces of paper make their way up to the bedroom. "Bring him down, along with the pictures," the lieutenant said. "Is that necessary?" Levyokin said. Why, did he have anything else to hide? the lieutenant snapped.

As they waited, Levyokin said that he hadn't given his foreman any hush money. On the contrary, they'd parked the three-tonner in the car park outside Oranienburg station, with the intention of having a beer at the kiosk. There he'd asked Joachim which of the two options he preferred: the foreign worker he was responsible for simply running away, or the foreign worker giving him a good thrashing before-hand. Joachim immediately plumped for the latter.

Laurenz Leithner, the farmer's brother, stood stooped in the doorway, three sheets of light-grey paper in his hand, and behind him, twice as wide, young Schwertfeger. "Show me," the lieutenant said. The man wandered over to the table and put two sheets of paper on it, the first with a broad yellow rectangle and above it a somewhat narrower red one, the other depicting a steel-blue triangle with a black point at the top. "What's that?" the lieutenant said. "A house and a castle," Leithner said, and Gollwitz said he could accept that at a pinch. "What about the third picture?" he asked. Laurenz Leithner raised his eyebrows at Levyokin, then put the third sheet of paper on top of those of the house and castle.

In the centre of the paper and set vertically was a white rectangle, bordered at the top by a strip of black, as wide as a thumb. Just below the centre was a small black square.

Schwertfeger, whose curiosity had made him approach the table, gazed at the picture for a while, then started to laugh. The colour had drained from the lieutenant's face.

Corporal Schwertfeger laughed, Levyokin looked at the floor and of course the most likely course of events was that the lieutenant would have gone over, grabbed Levyokin and dragged him to the table. There, shaking with anger, he would have pointed at the picture and said, "Is that what I think it is?" Levyokin would have said nothing at first, and then explained that Suprematist art was only ever what it was, no more and no less. He wasn't denying it then? the lieutenant would have asked, and Levyokin would have replied that the very essence of art was that it did not deny anything. The lieutenant would have torn a strip off Corporal Schwertfeger, telling him to stop laughing and say what he saw in the picture. Visibly shocked, Schwertfeger would have hummed and hawed, and finally said that the lieutenant mustn't be angry, but he didn't dare say.

The lieutenant would have sat down in his chair and

instructed the red-headed corporal to write the following:

Mikhail Yegorovich Levyokin, born on November 4th, 1919, in Udranka near Minsk, is a Russian prisoner of war who, by means of a cowardly escape, evaded his service to the German Volk. He misappropriated German property, in particular what was suspected to be precious artworks belonging to Reichsmarschall Hermann Göring, thereby causing damage which could no longer be quantified today. By using his language skills he tried to feign membership of a German ethnic group. Finally, under the pretext of producing supposed art, he proceeded to infect simple people with deviant and defeatist ideas, an undertaking that ultimately went so far as to sneer maliciously at the Führer. There could be no doubt, therefore, that Levyokin is guilty of desertion, stealing German property and undermining the will of the German Volk to fight. In accordance with the wartime criminal code and court martial statutes he has been sentenced to the most serious punishment. For the court martial, Lieutenant Bernd Gollwitz, March 31st, 1945.

The red-headed corporal would have written all this down as if someone were hot on his heels, and Corporal Schwertfeger would have stood beside Levyokin as if he'd been turned to stone. Levyokin himself would not have looked up again, not even in response to the lieutenant's question of whether there was anything else he would like to say. After that the lieutenant would have said, "Let's go, then."

Levyokin, the two corporals and the lieutenant would have walked along the house and the cart shed until they came to the last of the pear trees. There the lieutenant would have given the order: "Ready!" Because the red-headed corporal would have turned ghostly white and stood there as still as a statue, and Corporal Schwertfeger would have said, "I don't think he can, Lieutenant," Lieutenant Gollwitz would have taken out his pistol and shot Levyokin in the back of the neck.

That was the most likely course of events.

Later, Laurenz Leithner explained that he moved away from the table to make his way to the kitchen at the very moment when the lieutenant asked the fat corporal to say what he could see in the picture with the little black square in the middle. The last thing he heard was Schwertfeger's comment that he didn't dare say, as well as the sound of the lieutenant's boots on the parlour floor, as he was going around the table back to his chair. Laurenz asked the farmer's wife where her husband was and she said he was most likely filling the sowing machine outside by the coach house, for only half the summer barley had been broadcast so far.

And indeed Laurenz found his brother by the coach

house. The two of them just stood there briefly, the farmer in dark-blue overalls and he in his apron. He told his brother what had happened in the parlour, and in the end said that war made cowards of them all.

When they came out of the house, Levyokin between the two corporals and the lieutenant out in front, Jakob picked up the wooden shovel he'd been transferring grain with, approached the men and waited for them a few paces away from the trees. The lieutenant stopped, Laurenz said, and said nothing. Jakob put the shovel on the ground, looked the lieutenant in the eye and said, "Aren't you ashamed?"

The lieutenant returned the farmer's gaze for a few seconds. Then he grinned and slowly turned around, Laurenz said. He made a disdainful gesture in Levyokin's direction and said he should disappear. The Russian lifted his head briefly. Then he left, Laurenz said.

Half asleep, I realise that Annemarie is standing by my side of the bed. She's crying. "What's wrong?" I ask, and she says that she's wet the bed. "It doesn't matter," I say, "it's happened to me too." I climb out of bed. When she sees me reaching for the light switch she restrains me. "Please don't," she says. I take her hand and we go down to the kitchen together. But I've got to put the light on here, I say. She nods.

Her nightie is stuck to her thighs at both the front and back. "Take it off," I say. She hesitates. "Don't be ashamed," I say.

I take an enamel bowl from the lowest shelf in the cupboard and fill it with water from the large metal pitcher on the stove. It's still lukewarm. I plunge a dishcloth into the water, wring it out and wipe Annemarie where she's wet. She looks embarrassed and I think that there can hardly be anything that feels as good as she does, even through a dishcloth.

I know there's a pile of freshly washed old towels in the storeroom behind the pantry. I fetch a few of them. "What are you doing with those?" Annemarie asks. "Keeping you dry," I say. The linen cupboard is in the grandparents' bedroom, and I don't want to go in there right now. We leave her soaked nightie with the dirty washing and go back upstairs. I spread the towels across the bed, with a double layer in the middle. "Can you sleep without a nightie?" I ask. Annemarie nods. "Otherwise you can have mine," I say. "No, it's fine," she says.

She rolls onto her side and falls asleep immediately.

I lie awake the rest of the night, no idea why. It occurs to me that you can wet yourself when certain things happen and I think of how in the past few days Annemarie has barely asked if Agnes is going to adopt her. I think of the lieutenant's spectacles, of Antonia, who screamed for hours, and of St Lucy's eyes, and I think of how nice it is if someone else is there, and how bad if someone's no longer there, no matter whether it's wartime or not. At a certain point I keep thinking the same thing until dawn begins to break outside. Then I know what I have to do.

I slip out of bed and get dressed, knickers, vest, tights, green-and-black checked smock, woollen jacket. The dark-brown shoes that are too small for Katharina. I take Annemarie's satchel out from under the bed, empty it and put in my brown notebooks and the pencils. She would understand. I don't have anything else to carry these things in. When I leave the bedroom she's sleeping deeply.

A blackbird is singing outside. It ought to shut up. I don't like blackbirds. As I walk past the cart shed I close my eyes.

Like a small child, I think – nothing happened, nothing at all. When I open them again I see there's nothing beneath the pear trees anymore, no haycart, no slurry barrel, neither of the two ploughs.

I climb up to the hayloft, make my way to the very back and reach down along the planks until I feel the oilcloth. I pull up the long object, stick it under my armpit and climb down again. Once outside the barn I hang the satchel on my back, then the rolled-up picture.

I give the cart shed a wide berth, then walk diagonally across the field until I come to the path by a bank of hazelnut bushes. I follow it until I get to the ditch, where I turn around several times. It's childish, I know, but I'd like to see the roof of the farmhouse disappear.

As soon as it's gone and the fire pond comes into view, I know I'm at the right place. I step onto the strip of meadow beside the pond, take the things off my back and start untying the ribbons that fasten the roll. When I fold back the oilcloth, tiny grains of blue trickle over my fingers. Instinctively I recoil, as if it were poison.

The picture is stiffer than I'd expected, so I look for some large stones by the pond. After unfurling the first dozen or so centimetres I put the stones on the flat edge. Then it gets easier.

First I see a white, orange and green rainbow. Then a blue horse's head. Behind that a second horse's head, this time more orange. Beneath these, two more blue horses. The one at the front has a dark-blue crescent on its chest. To the left some hills in green and red.

There are some things you don't expect – squadrons of aircraft in the sky, stories about martyrs, how good someone can feel, or somebody reciting a ballad. Sometimes you don't expect the wickedness people are capable of, nor a picture in which four horses piled on top of each other are shining like a hundred burning oil trains.

I'm squatting on my heels beside a small dark pond, and there are two things I know. First, that paintings must be just like this – like a hundred burning oil trains – and second, that Mikhail Levyokin didn't paint this picture. But maybe he stole it.

A little later I'm still sitting on the strip of meadow, writing in one of my brown notebooks. Besides the stories, I write what I've been writing about all the time recently: a derailed train and a girl lying in this train, covered by other people. I have only a few sentences, they don't go anywhere and I've no idea why I'm writing them.

I'm equally at a loss as to where I might go now or what I'll do next. If anybody asks me who I am, I'll tell them it's in my books. That much I know. Maybe I'll also tell them that my name is Nelli. But that's not necessary.

The Story of
the Happy Ending

They had moved away from the pear trees and dug the pit in the middle of the meadow, perhaps ten metres from the coach house. Despite this they encountered all manner of roots. Four of them worked together, taking turns to dig, the farmer, his brother and the two corporals. All told they got to a depth of a metre and a half quite rapidly. Corporal Schwertfeger, in particular, really put his back into it. Lieutenant Gollwitz, who supervised the operation, said he dug like an animal, but he didn't expect anything else of a Bavarian. Schwertfeger gave the impression that he hadn't heard a thing.

It was just after the lieutenant reckoned that they'd gone far enough and didn't need to dig any deeper that Laurenz Leithner laid his spade up on the grass, climbed out of the pit and told the lieutenant that he felt cold and had to put something else on. "Cold?" the lieutenant said, and Leithner said, yes, he was permanently freezing, he had it on his lungs.

Laurenz climbed the stairs to his room. He was indeed shivering, and before he opened the door he had to negotiate a coughing fit.

He pulled open the middle drawer of his bureau and took out two envelopes, one light brown, the other white. With his tongue he moistened the tip of an indelible pencil, crossed out the "W" in the upper right-hand corner of the white envelope, and wrote LAURENZ JOSEF LEITHNER, LAST WILL AND TESTAMENT in the middle. Then he took a letter from the light-brown envelope bearing the stamp of the German Wehrmacht, unfolded it and placed it beside the white envelope on the desktop of the bureau. Besides the Wehrmacht stamp, the letter had another one, depicting a greyhound running across a meadow.

Laurenz Leithner went to his wardrobe, took the grey felt coat from its hanger to the very left of the rail and put it on. Before leaving the room, he slipped the empty envelope with the Wehrmacht stamp into his outer coat pocket.

The three others had made good progress filling in the pit. Schwertfeger and the farmer were stamping down the earth on top, and the red-headed corporal smoothed it with the blade of his shovel.

Laurenz Leithner went up to the lieutenant, took the envelope from his coat pocket and said he had something to show him. Noticing the Wehrmacht stamp, Lieutenant Gollwitz asked what it was about. With a discreet nod of his head in the direction of his brother, Laurenz Leithner said under his breath that this was something he could only talk about in private.

"Feeling warmer now?" the lieutenant asked as the two of them wandered along the side of the barn, and Laurenz said, yes, thank you.

The rear wall of the barn faced westwards and so was in the shade. The lieutenant brought the envelope up to his face so he could take a closer look at the stamp.

In the few seconds during which the lieutenant frowned, felt inside the envelope, looked confused then raised his head, Laurenz Leithner took the sawn-off shotgun from the inside pocket of his coat, cocked the hammers and aimed the barrels at the lieutenant's stomach, just below the breastbone.

Later, Laurenz Leithner said that before he pulled the triggers, the lieutenant just managed to utter the words, "That's not loaded."

Afterwards the red-headed corporal began to cry, and Schwertfeger pointed at the pit they'd only just filled in, saying, "But we're not going to put him in there."

The four of them carried the lieutenant up to the house, along the south side of the animal sheds. The farmer fetched a crowbar and used it to lift the concrete cover of the old lime pit. Before they dropped the lieutenant into it, Laurenz said, the red-headed corporal asked, "His spectacles too?"

Nobody laughed.

PAULUS HOCHGATTERER is a writer and child psychiatrist living in Vienna. He is the author of several novels and story collections, including *The Sweetness of Life* (for which he was the Austrian winner of the European Literature Prize) and *The Mattress House*, two crime novels published by MacLehose Press. For this novel he was shortlisted for the Austrian Book Prize in 2018.

JAMIE BULLOCH is the translator of novels by Timur Vermes, Steven Uhly, F. C. Delius, Daniela Krien, Jörg Fauser, Martin Suter, Roland Schimmelpfennig and Oliver Bottini. For his translation of Birgit Vanderbeke's *The Mussel Feast* he was the winner of the Schlegel–Tieck Prize.